Just a big baby . . .

"We can't just leave you!" Tash argued.

"This is our fight, Tash," Luke said calmly. "Vader is more powerful than you can imagine. You've got to get out of here. We'll hold the Imperials off as long as we can."

Hoole shook his head. "We cannot allow you to risk your lives on our account."

"Hey, risking my life for other people's problems has become a hobby," Han smirked.

Leia pointed to four of the Rebel commandos. "Sikes! Bergan! Tino! Meex! Front and center!"

The four commandos hustled forward. "You guys have a new assignment. Get these civilians safely back to the ships. If we haven't joined you in four hours, blast off this planet and don't look back."

"Yes, Your Highness!" said the commandos.

"We're leaving," Hoole said. "Where's the child?"

"I hid him over here where it was safe from the blaster fire," Zak said. "He's right behind this rock."

Zak stepped behind the rock, and gasped.

The baby was now a little boy.

Look for a preview of Star Wars: Galaxy of Fear #7, *The Brain Spiders,* in the back of this book!

STAR WARS®
GALAXY of FEAR

BOOK 6

ARMY OF
TERROR

JOHN WHITMAN

BANTAM BOOKS
NEW YORK · TORONTO · LONDON · SYDNEY · AUCKLAND

To George Lucas, and to the Star Wars writers and fans who made these books possible.

RL 6.0, 008–012

ARMY OF TERROR

A Bantam Skylark Book / October 1997

ISBN 0-553-48455-9

Published simultaneously in the United States and Canada.

Bantam Books are published by Bantam Books, a division of Bantam Doubleday Dell Publishing Group, Inc. Its trademark, consisting of the words "Bantam Books" and the portrayal of a rooster, is Registered in U.S. Patent and Trademark Office and in other countries. Marca Registrada. Bantam Books, 1540 Broadway, New York, New York 10036.

PRINTED IN THE UNITED STATES OF AMERICA
OPM 0 9 8 7 6 5 4 3 2 1

PROLOGUE

The small shuttle craft glided through space toward an enormous Star Destroyer. The shuttle was tiny compared to the large battleship. It looked like a speck of dust floating through the void.

But thousands of soldiers on board the powerful Star Destroyer trembled in fear when they heard the name of the shuttle's single passenger.

Darth Vader.

Vader did not watch as his shuttle landed in the Destroyer's docking bay. He was deep in his own dark thoughts. One phrase worked its way into his mind.

Project Starscream.

Months ago, Starscream had been a promising experiment run by the Imperial scientist Borborygmus Gog. Now it was all but ruined, thanks to the interference of a scientist named Hoole and two meddling children. They had successfully wrecked the first five phases of Starscream. They had tampered with D'vouran, the living planet. They had destroyed the undead research on Necropolis. They had neutralized the plague virus on Gobindi, and then demolished the promising Nightmare Machine. Finally, they had shattered Gog's plans to manipulate the power of the Force.

Vader clenched a gloved fist. Gog had hidden this last plan from the Dark Lord. Vader knew the scientist feared him and had searched for a way to cancel out Vader's dark side powers. *Fortunately for Gog,* Vader thought, *he died*

1

before I discovered his plan. I would have made him beg for death.

Hoole and his young companions had escaped from Nespis 8 just before Vader arrived. Even now, Vader's ships were combing the nearby star systems in search of the escapees.

Leaving the shuttle, Vader barely acknowledged the presence of the stormtrooper squadron that saluted him as he strode from his shuttle, his dark cape swirling behind him. He did not pause until he reached the captain of the Star Destroyer, who bowed nervously.

"Lord Vader," the captain said. "Welcome aboard. The ship is yours to command."

"Excellent, Captain," Vader hissed through his black, skull-like mask.

Vader continued walking. The captain struggled to keep up with the Dark Lord's powerful stride. "I—I trust your mission to Nespis 8 went well?"

"It is not yet complete," Vader replied. "I have one thing more to do before Project Starscream is completely under my control."

Vader knew the scout ships would not find Hoole and his companions. But he did know where Hoole would go next. He felt the dark side of the Force flow through him. He knew many things. He could not see the future clearly, but he sensed that it would end in bloodshed. He relished the thought.

"My lord," the captain asked. "What are your orders?"

"Tell the scout ships to continue their search," Vader commanded. "Meanwhile, set your course for the headquarters of Project Starscream."

Vader flexed the fingers of his right hand. Yes, blood would be shed. He was sure of it.

And he would be the one to shed it.

CHAPTER 1

"There's another one," Tash Arranda said with a tremor in her voice.

She pointed at a control panel in the cockpit of the *Shroud*. The scanner registered a tiny blip hovering just at the edge of their sensor range.

On her left, her brother Zak held his breath. On her right, her uncle Hoole sat as still as stone. Only his tight grip on the *Shroud*'s guidance control stick revealed his tension.

All three of them knew what that blip represented—an Imperial Star Destroyer, bristling with weapons. It was like an enormous shark, hunting through the vast ocean of space.

It was hunting for them.

Tash let her breath out slowly. Only the *Shroud*'s emergency lights were running, but even in their dim glow she could see her breath in the cold air of the *Shroud*'s cockpit. Twenty minutes before, Hoole had deactivated almost all of the ship's power systems, and he had turned the life support down to a bare minimum.

"I'm freezing," Tash muttered. "Can't we turn the heat up a little?"

"Well, it's warmer in an Imperial detention center," Zak replied. "Which is where we'll find ourselves if we power up the systems and they detect us."

"Here it comes," Hoole said flatly.

They watched as the blip changed course, growing larger as it headed straight for them.

"Do they see us?" Zak asked in a sharp whisper.

"I don't know," Hoole replied.

"Maybe we should make a break for it."

"No, it's too late," Hoole said. "We are under their guns. We will just have to wait it out."

Tash looked at her uncle. He stared stonily at the ship's instruments. For once, she admired his inhuman ability to stay levelheaded. Hoole was a Shi'ido and, unlike his human niece and nephew, he seemed able to disconnect his emotions from his surroundings. His face rarely changed expression.

The blip grew so large that it seemed to blot out the scanning screen. Tash and Zak felt the *Shroud* begin to shake around them.

Zak, Tash, their uncle Hoole, and his droid, D-V9, had been on the run from Imperial forces for two days, ever since they had fled from the space station Nespis 8 and Borborygmus Gog.

Tash shivered when she remembered Nespis 8 and Gog. Gog was a Shi'ido, like Uncle Hoole, and could change his form at will. He was also an Imperial scientist. By shapeshifting into disguise, Gog had been able to lure Tash, Zak, and Hoole to Nespis 8. And when the evil scientist realized he could not use Tash's sensitivity to the Force in his experiments, he had almost killed her. But Gog, who had come so close to destroying them all, had fallen to his own death down a deep shaft in the space station.

Unfortunately, their troubles had not ended with Gog's death. The scientist had created Project Starscream for the Empire, and the Emperor's most powerful servant had come to Nespis 8 to investigate. Tash, Zak, Hoole, and Deevee had escaped Nespis 8 just before the arrival of Darth Vader.

Vader. The thought of him made Tash's skin crawl. He was the Dark Lord of the Sith, a master of the dark side of the Force and, next to the Emperor, the most powerful man in the galaxy. He was far more terrifying than Gog. They said Vader could kill people with a single thought. They also said that, rather than kill, the Dark Lord preferred to rule through two devices: torture and terror. None of them wanted to imagine what horrors would await them in one of Vader's prison cells.

In the viewport, the two Arrandas saw space rocks of

various sizes zip by. Hoole had attempted to hide their ship from the Imperials by flying through a small asteroid belt and landing the *Shroud* on an asteroid twice its size.

Suddenly, Zak cried out. "It's going to pass right over us!"

A giant field of white had settled over their ship, blotting out the stars. They were looking at the underbelly of an Imperial Star Destroyer. The floating fortress was gigantic. Tash saw a squad of Imperial TIE fighters buzz like angry flies around the massive cruiser's docking port. Tash and Zak knew that sensor beams were shooting from the Star Destroyer, searching for any sign of them. But because Hoole had cut off all the *Shroud*'s power, their ship was as dead as the asteroid on which it floated. The Imperial sensor beams passed over it without stopping.

The energy put out by the Star Destroyer's enormous engines shook the entire asteroid upon which they sat. The *Shroud* trembled like a leaf on a tree. For a moment Zak thought the energy waves would tear the ship apart. But a moment later, the giant battleship had passed on. Zak and Tash sighed and looked at each other. They were safe.

"I am going to power up the systems so that we can depart," Uncle Hoole said. "Please see how Deevee's repairs are coming along."

"Power up?" Zak asked. "Where are we going?"

Hoole paused. A frown pulled at the edge of his mouth. Hoole rarely explained to Tash and Zak what he was planning and where they were going. But this time, his expression seemed to suggest that Zak and Tash had a right to know.

"We are going to end this mystery once and for all," the Shi'ido declared. "I know where Project Starscream is located."

CHAPTER 2

"What!" Zak shouted in surprise

"H-How?" Tash stammered. "Where?"

Hoole looked at them closely before speaking. "I found some data stored in the computers on Nespis 8. It suggested that the main headquarters for Gog's experiment are on the planet Kiva. It's only a short hyperspace jump from here, and I want to go there and make sure everything Gog was doing is destroyed."

"But—But what if we run into other Imperial scientists there?" Zak stammered.

"We won't," Hoole promised. "Trust me."

Stunned, Zak and Tash could only stare as Hoole added, "Now please make sure that Deevee is fully operational."

Before Zak and Tash could ask any more questions, their uncle had already glided past them.

Zak and Tash were still shaking their heads as they reached the small maintenance room at the center of their starship. The door to the room slid back, revealing a tall, humanlike droid. DV-9's once-silver body was covered with scratches and soot, and several dents pockmarked his metallic shell. A long, black streak ran across his chestplate. The droid had obviously tried to polish it away, but the scar could still be seen in the cabin lights.

"How are the repairs going, Deevee?" Zak asked.

The droid sighed heavily. "Well enough, I suppose. I've corrected all the internal damage that blaster bolt caused, but I'm afraid I'll bear this scar forever."

"I'm sorry, Deevee," Tash said sincerely. Deevee was the one who had saved her from Gog. He had jumped in front of a bolt from Gog's blaster meant for her. "If it weren't for you, I'd be nothing but a vapor cloud back in that space station."

Deevee sniffed. "Think no more of it, Tash. I was doing my duty as your caretaker." He looked at his battered body and sighed again. "Besides, although my outer shell has become rather unsightly, that blaster would have done you far more harm than it did me. Now, if it had been an ion cannon, that would have been another story."

"Ion cannon?" Tash asked.

Zak, a starship engine and weapon fanatic, jumped in. "An ion cannon attacks circuitry and electronics. Blasters

10

just punch their way into whatever they hit. But ion weapons can really shred computers and servos.''

Suddenly, the *Shroud*'s power systems kicked in. Tash and Zak blinked and Deevee readjusted his photoreceptors as the main lights came on and the ship began to hum with energy. Seconds later, without warning, the *Shroud* lurched away from its asteroid hideout and pushed its way into open space.

''Weird,'' Tash noted. ''He must be in a hurry. He didn't even ask us to strap ourselves in.''

Zak shook his head. ''Figures. The one time he tells us where we're going, he finds some other way to be mysterious.''

''Where *are* we going?'' Deevee asked, as he tried to close a small panel on his chestplate.

Zak helped him close his chest panel. ''Uncle Hoole says he's figured out where Gog's headquarters are. He's taking us there now. Someplace called Kiva.''

The droid tilted his head to the side. ''Kiva? How fascinating. I've wanted to visit Kiva from the moment my anthropology research program was installed!''

''What's there?'' Tash asked.

''Nothing!'' Deevee said excitedly. ''Well, to be precise, there's nothing there anymore.'' The droid slipped into his teacher mode, which meant a lecture was coming. He began: ''Kiva is an example of how science can do great harm if caution is not taken. Years ago, there was a thriving cul-

11

ture on Kiva. The Kivans were known as the best artists and builders in the galaxy. There was also an Imperial base there, where scientists conducted secret biological experiments.''

''Experiments,'' Tash groaned. ''I've had enough of experiments, thanks.''

''What kind of experiments?'' Zak asked. He soaked up technological information like a sponge. But he was disappointed by Deevee's response.

''No one knows. The experiments were being conducted by a scientist named Mammon, but no one ever found out just what he was doing on Kiva. What we do know is that whatever he was doing went terribly wrong. There was some sort of accident, and the entire civilization on Kiva was wiped out.'' Deevee paused to let the terrible information sink in.

''Wiped out,'' Tash repeated sadly. ''Kind of like Alderaan.''

Zak nodded. The two Arrandas understood how terrible the loss of an entire planet could be. Their homeworld, Alderaan, had been destroyed by the Emperor's Death Star only eight months before. The Arrandas had lost their parents, their home, and their friends, all in one terrible moment.

Deevee continued. ''The scientist, Mammon, was condemned by everyone, even the Emperor. He went into hiding and has never been heard from again. The planet became barren and the entire civilization of Kiva was lost.''

"Maybe that's why Gog decided to build his headquarters there," Zak suggested. "Who would bother to look on a planet everyone knew was deserted?"

"Maybe," Tash agreed. She was kind of glad the place they were going was deserted, after everything they'd been through on Nespis 8. She remembered that Nespis 8 was supposedly abandoned—but they'd had plenty of surprises there. Who knew what awaited them on Kiva? "Come on, let's get to the cockpit and help Uncle Hoole," she said to Zak.

Deevee's battered body whined a little as he walked, but otherwise he functioned normally as all three hurried back to the ship's control room. They offered to help, but Hoole had their course all set. There was little to do for the next few hours but watch the white, blurred lights of hyperspace rush past.

Finally, with a frown on his face, Hoole powered down the hyperdrive, and a planet the color of charcoal appeared before them.

"Kiva," Hoole said stiffly. "Don't worry, we will not be detected. This planet is lifeless."

"We know," Zak said. "Deevee told us all about Mammon."

Hoole raised an eyebrow at his droid. Anger crossed his usually unreadable face. "I would have thought you had better ways to waste your time than teaching them about dead planets."

Deevee was startled. "Master Hoole, I—"

13

"Never mind," Hoole snapped. "We're entering orbit."

Zak and Tash exchanged a quick glance. They had rarely heard Hoole snap at Deevee, and never when the droid was trying to teach them something.

The great ball of dark gray matter that was Kiva filled the entire viewscreen as the ship drew nearer. Tash stared down at the dark world, amazed at how barren it looked. Suddenly, a wave of fear swept through her like a warning.

"What's that?" she said, stabbing a finger at the viewscreen.

"What's what?" Zak asked, alarmed by the fear in her voice.

"That!" Tash said again.

Then they all saw it. On the planet's surface, something glowed with sudden brightness. It was tiny, but clearly visible even hundreds of kilometers above the surface.

A sensor alarm bleeped. "Energy readings just went off the scale," Zak yelped.

"Something's attacking us!" Tash cried.

"Taking evasive action," Hoole responded, banking the *Shroud* hard to the right.

Too late.

An enormous energy beam streaked toward them, slamming into the ship with the light of a dozen suns. The *Shroud* spun to the right, and continued to spin even after the bright light vanished. Tash felt her stomach leap into her throat. They were falling. The ship lurched into a nosedive, and Tash was slammed against a wall. Through the

14

spinning viewport, she could see the planet spiraling up-ward toward them.

"What's happening?" she yelled.

"No power," Hoole said. He was straining forward in the pilot's seat, trying to regain control of the ship. "We're out of control. We're going to crash!"

CHAPTER

We're going to die. That same thought gripped both Tash's and Zak's minds at the same time.

Neither one of them could speak. Their mouths and throats had gone dry, and all they could do was watch the surface of the planet grow closer by the second.

Zak knew there were procedures to regain ship control. There were steps to follow. But he was too terrified to remember them. Then he heard a calm voice speak over the sound of the atmosphere rushing past the ship's hull.

"Restarting repulsor engines," Hoole said aloud. "No response. Main circuits are off-line."

The planet's surface was very near now, but Hoole's voice was utterly calm. "Switching to backup circuit board." Zak heard something click. But it was too late. The planet rushed up to crush them. "Circuits are on-line. Restarting repulsor engines again."

A low groan rumbled through the ship. "Brace yourselves!" Hoole warned. "Engaging thrusters."

The ship's forward repulsors fired up, breaking against the overwhelming pull of gravity. Tash and Zak were thrown forward, slamming into the *Shroud*'s main console.

"By the Maker!" Deevee cried as he toppled over the copilot's chair. "I just put myself back together!"

The ship continued to fall, but it also began to slow down as Hoole gained more control.

"We're going to make it!" Tash cried.

"Not quite," Hoole said grimly. "Hold on."

Try as he would, he couldn't pull the ship out of its dive. All he could do was adjust the angle of their fall so they wouldn't slam right into the ground. The *Shroud* hit the surface of Kiva like a rock thrown across the surface of a lake— skipping once, twice, three times—then plowing over a rocky field as parts of the hull were torn off the ship's frame. The ship scraped across jagged mounds of stone that gouged long cuts into the tough metal.

Inside, the four passengers were thrown around. The room was filled with flying debris as equipment, datachips, holodisks, and everything else not tied down suddenly leaped into the air. Tash felt a datachip bounce off her forehead with the force of a small rocket. A moment later she blinked as a trickle of blood dripped into her left eye.

Finally, the ship came to rest.

Before Tash and Zak could climb to their feet, Hoole was standing over them. "No broken bones, no serious wounds," he said to each of them, then pressed a piece of cloth against Tash's cut. "Can you stand?"

They both nodded and the Shi'ido helped them up, then quickly turned to Deevee. "Are you functioning?"

Servos whined as the droid climbed to his feet. "It seems to defy the laws of physics," Deevee said, "but I'm still operational."

"Good," Hoole said, as though they hadn't just had a very close brush with death. "Please go check the engines for damage."

With that, Hoole began to check the cockpit equipment. Tash held the cloth against her forehead and watched her uncle. She had to admire his calm. Her hands were still shaking from the crash, but Hoole was steady as a rock, running checks on all the systems.

"Oh, this is *not* prime," she heard Zak mutter.

Zak was looking at the floor just outside the cockpit. There was a gaping hole in the metal floorboards. It was so wide and deep that they could see straight through to the gray rock of the planet's surface. "I think this ship just found its permanent home," Zak said. "It sure isn't going to fly anywhere soon."

"I am afraid Zak is right," Hoole confirmed. "There are at least four major holes in the hull too big to repair. The crash took out almost every system, including the navicomputer. Even if the engines worked, we could not fly. This ship is dead.''

They were marooned.

A short while later, Zak, Tash, Deevee, and Hoole stood outside what was left of the *Shroud*. Each of them carried a small supply of food and water salvaged from the ship's galley, and Hoole pulled an emergency crash kit out of the wreckage. It contained two small tents and a cooking unit.

Zak had also insisted on bringing along as many of the ship's datachips as possible. The *Shroud*'s computer banks had been full of interesting information.

"It was a good ship," Zak sighed. "It got us through a lot of scrapes."

"Funny," Tash added. "This ship started out as part of Gog's plan. Now it's as if we've brought it home to him."

Zak nodded unhappily at the memory of how they found the ship. The *Shroud* had belonged to one of Gog's henchman, another evil scientist named Evazan.

Hoole said, "Come. It's not a long walk, but we should start at once."

"Where are we going?" Zak asked.

"Just follow me," Hoole said.

The direction Hoole chose seemed no better or worse than any other. In fact, every direction looked the same. Kiva was absolutely dead, made up of kilometer after kilometer of dark gray rock under a roof of dark gray sky. Even the sun looked gray. The light was dim, but strong enough for huge, jagged pillars of rock to cast long shadows on the dry ground.

Zak stood next to one rock that was taller than he was. "These things look like giant teeth."

"Or frozen people," Tash added. "They're all over the place. Like millions of people, turned into rock."

"Be silent," Hoole warned sharply. Tash and Zak looked at each other and shrugged.

There was no sound, other than a sad wind that moaned through the rocks. Zak looked around. Something bothered him. But what was it? Then it hit him.

"No life," he muttered. He crouched down and stared at the ground, looking for the tiniest sign of growing things, a weed, or even a thorn. "There's nothing here. Not even a blade of grass."

"You're right, Zak," his sister replied. "This place makes Tatooine seem like a garden paradise."

"Well I hope there's *something* here," Zak said. "If we don't get help, or a ship, we're going to end up just like this place. Lifeless."

Tash pointed at Hoole, striding ahead of them. The Shi'ido had been traveling along at a steady pace since they stepped off the ship. "Well, he seems to think there's something here. How does he even know where we're going?"

Neither of them could answer that question.

Although Hoole had ordered them to be silent, Deevee chattered happily. "Master Hoole, this is a rare opportunity indeed!'' the droid said as they hiked. ''Why, you must know that there has been no serious study of the planet Kiva. Although I did read a paper once by an anthropologist from Circarpous 4 . . .''

Tash stopped listening. A motion caught her eye. It was small—but on a planet with absolutely no life, she noticed it right away. She thought she'd seen something step from behind one of the rocks. But when she turned to get a better look, all she saw was the rock's own shadow. She shrugged.

''. . . and according to the articles I've read,'' Deevee went on, ''the Kivans may have left behind entire cities in the aftermath of Mammon's disaster . . .''

''I believe that is enough background, Deevee,'' Hoole said shortly.

''But, Master Hoole, surely you appreciate how interesting this planet must be to an anthropologist! It's a dead civilization.''

''I know. I *am* an anthropologist,'' Hoole snapped. But he said nothing more.

A moment later something caught Tash's eye again. But when she turned again to look, there was nothing but shadows. For a moment, she thought she could see the shadows stretching toward them. But then she realized it was only the setting sun, making the shadows grow longer on the ground. Still, something had caught her eye . . .

''Uncle Hoole,'' she asked, ''is it possible that there's still something alive here?''

"No," Hoole said definitely. "Every living thing on Kiva died."

"But I thought I saw something—"

"A trick of the light," the Shi'ido interrupted.

"But something fired at us," Zak said. "There's got to be someone here."

"Not someone. Something," Hoole said as they came to the top of a small hill. "Look."

On the other side of the hill, nestled in a small, barren valley, stood a large tower. An ion cannon was mounted atop the tower, its tip pointing up into the gray sky. The tower hummed with energy as it swiveled automatically on its base.

They walked down into the valley. Here, the shadows were even thicker.

"It is a computerized defense system," Hoole explained. "It's fully automated."

"How did you know that?" Tash asked.

Hoole shrugged. "The sensors picked it up just before we were hit." The Shi'ido looked at his niece and nephew. "So, as you can see, we are quite alone on this planet."

Uncle Hoole always has an explanation for everything, thought Tash, as she wandered away from him and Zak. She picked her way through the maze of toothlike rocks toward the ion tower. *It's so much darker here in the valley*—Tash couldn't believe how fast the shadows moved here. As

22

Zak's and Hoole's voices faded in the distance, Tash stood still, looking all around her, trying to see just how the rocks cast such weird, fast-moving shadows.

Suddenly, Tash screamed. Something had grabbed her by both wrists—she was being attacked!

CHAPTER

"Help!" Tash cried out.

Zak, Hoole, and Deevee ran toward the sound of her voice. But once they found her, all they could see were shadows cast by the rocks and Tash struggling with something invisible.

"Get it off me!" Tash yelled.

"What?" Deevee asked.

"The shad—!" she began. Then she was sucked into the darkness.

"Tash!" Zak yelled. He started forward, but stumbled. His foot had caught on something. Looking down, he saw that as he'd rushed forward, he had stepped into a shadow. Now his foot was stuck.

Hoole and Deevee had charged toward Tash, too, but seeing Zak, they stopped.

"What's wrong, Zak?" Hoole asked.

"I don't know," Zak said. He tugged at his foot, but it wouldn't budge. "Something's got me." He tugged again.

This time, something tugged back.

Zak was dragged forward into the shadow. In an instant, day turned into night. It wasn't the pitch-blackness of late night, but more like the darkness of evening, just after sunset. Zak could see the ground, he could see the sky, he could even see Hoole and Deevee, but everything lay under a shadowy shroud. His uncle and Deevee were moving their arms frantically, and they seemed to be shouting, but Zak couldn't hear them. He called out to them, but he could tell that they couldn't hear him either. It was as if a dark, heavy curtain had dropped between them.

Mammon!

The word was whispered close to him, so close he felt something brush against his ear. Turning quickly, Zak saw only more shadows.

Mammon!

A second voice moaned in his other ear.

Zak turned again, and again saw nothing but shadows around him. A little farther away, deeper in the strange bubble of darkness, he saw his sister lying huddled on the ground. Zak started toward her, but every step took immense effort. It was like walking through a thick goo. It felt as though many hands were pushing against him, keeping him from getting near Tash.

"Tash!" he called out.

Tash lifted her head slowly.

"Zak . . . ," she said weakly.

Mammonmammonmammonmammonmammon!

Angry voices swirled around Zak like a moaning wind, all of them repeating that same name over and over.

"Stop it!" Zak shouted, plugging his ears. "Leave us alone!"

Murderer! the voices cried.

"What?" Zak wasn't sure he had heard right.

Murderermurderermurderermurderermurderer!

"Who are you? What do you want?" he called out.

To his surprise, Tash answered him. She had managed to sit up and look at him through the fog. "They're angry, Zak," she mumbled. "They're so angry."

"Who?" he asked.

Something hard and sharp lashed out at Zak from the darkness, shredding the front of his tunic and just missing his skin. Something had attacked him from the darkness. No, not something *from* the darkness, he realized. The darkness itself had attacked him!

"Help!" he shouted in panic. "Help!"

A moment later Hoole charged forward. As he did, the Shi'ido changed shape. The flesh crawled across his bones and an instant later Hoole had vanished, replaced by a huge, hairy bantha, its four legs pounding the ground and its sharp tusks raking the air as it charged.

The bantha crashed into the wall of darkness, storming

straight at Zak. The bantha reared up, searching for enemies to strike.

But all that could be seen was darkness, and all that could be heard were the whispering voices as they moaned more ferociously than ever.

Mammon! Murderer! Mammon! Murderer! M-U-R-D-E-R-E-R!

The bantha paused. Its front feet came crashing down to the ground. It shivered violently, and a moment later Hoole returned to his normal shape. But he kept shaking, as though he were freezing cold.

"Uncle Hoole?" Zak called out. "Are you all right?"

Hoole fell to his knees, still shivering. He covered his face with his hands. "Oh, no," Zak heard his uncle mutter. "Oh . . . no."

Hoole's entrance into the ring of shadows had triggered something in the darkness. The shadows began to take a more solid shape. Zak could make out vaguely humanoid figures. He saw heads and arms the color of shadow, with bodies that melted into the darkness. They swarmed around Hoole and the two Arrandas, snarling the same words over and over.

Mammon!

Murderer!

"We've got to get out of here!" Zak yelled to his sister and uncle. Neither of them responded.

The creatures closed in. Through the gloom, Zak thought

27

he saw dark claws reach out to grab Hoole's throat. He expected Hoole to shapeshift into something large and fierce that could tear the weird creatures to shreds, but Hoole didn't even move.

Dark claws clutched at the Shi'ido's throat.

Suddenly, an energy blast tore through the darkness and slammed into the ground, turning the ring of shadows into a bright circle of light. Tiny bolts of lightning leaped up from the spot where the energy bolt had struck, wrapping themselves around the shadow creatures. Frightened screams filled the air, and then all the shadows fled.

Blinking from the bright light, Zak watched them go. The dark bubble burst, and the shadows slipped away into cracks in the rocks, shrinking until they vanished.

Deevee appeared at Zak's side. "Thank the Maker I managed to drive them off!" the droid said. "Are you all right?"

"What . . ." Zak tried to speak. "How . . . ?"

"The ion cannon." Deevee pointed to the big laser tower. The cannon was now pointing directly at them. "It was the only large weapon within reach. I managed to override its automatic program and point it toward you, hoping it would frighten those creatures away."

Zak had to admire Deevee's cleverness. An ion weapon, since it only attacked electronic circuitry, would not do much damage to people. But it sure made a lot of light and noise!

28

"It did more than scare them," Zak said, remembering how they had screamed. "I think it hurt them."

By the time he had finished speaking, both Hoole and Tash were on their feet. Tash looked really upset. "I could feel them through the Force," she said. "Whatever they are, they're full of hate."

"No kidding," Zak replied, tugging at his torn shirt. "I could tell that *without* the Force. What were they?" he asked, looking at Hoole.

Hoole's face was very pale, and his eyes were still wide. It was the first time Zak or Tash could remember him looking at all afraid. Their uncle was obviously trying to hide his feeling, but he couldn't. In a hoarse voice, Hoole said, "I do not know. But I'm sure that . . . it is not important to us."

"They kept saying the name 'Mammon,' " Zak remembered. "That's that scientist who destroyed this place, isn't it?"

"It is," Deevee replied, tilting his silver head. "That is most curious. I wonder"—he looked at Hoole—"could these beings, these wraiths, possibly be related to the original inhabitants of this planet?"

"Perhaps. It does not concern us," Hoole said. "Come. We should leave before they return. Our destination is very close."

Hoole turned away and started toward the far end of the little valley. The others followed slowly behind.

"Did you see him?" Zak whispered to his sister. "I've *never* seen Hoole act like that."

Tash nodded. "I don't know what's going on, but it has something to do with those . . . those 'wraiths.' Isn't that what Deevee called them?" She shuddered. "I'm telling you, Zak, they were furious. And their fury was directed right at us!"

"Why us?" Zak replied. "We've never done anything to them. We've never even been here before—"

"I have a theory," Deevee interrupted him. "Perhaps these creatures somehow survived the accident that destroyed their species. Maybe they call all offworlders 'Mammon.' "

"You could be right," Zak agreed, looking back at the valley. "But I hope I never see them again to find out."

They followed Hoole for another kilometer over the rocky terrain. As before, Uncle Hoole seemed to know exactly where he was going. He led them along winding paths in the hills, and through fields of tall, narrow rocks that rose from the ground like stone trees. Finally, they came to a narrow passage that led into a cliff. As they entered, they could see that they were in a dead-end canyon. At the far end of the canyon, Zak and Tash saw a large building that seemed to grow out of the stone itself.

The entrance to the fortress was a large durasteel door. It looked impossible to open. But to their surprise, Hoole walked up to the control panel, punched in a security code, and watched as the door slid back with a soft *whoosh*.

"Just how much information did you find back on Nespis 8?" Tash asked him.

"Enough," the Shi'ido answered, stepping into the dark hallway beyond.

There were several chambers, and corridors leading off in many directions, but again, Hoole knew exactly where he was going. He led the others down a long corridor that led to the heart of the fortress, a large chamber in the center. In this chamber was an enormous command chair. Beside it was a control console, and above that was a row of viewscreens.

"Is this—Is this really Gog's headquarters?" Tash whispered. "Is this where Project Starscream was created?"

"Yes," Hoole said. He walked to the far end of the room, where there was another door, but this time, when he punched a combination into the security panel, the door failed to open.

"Deevee," the Shi'ido called. "The power to this room is shut down."

"I'll take care of it, Master Hoole," the droid replied. Approaching the control console, Deevee studied it for a moment and then ran his metal hands over a series of controls. Moments later, there was a loud hum as the room's power systems started. The viewscreens lit up. But the monitors showed nothing but static.

"That's going to tell us a lot," Zak said.

"I shall see if I can make repairs," Deevee said. He punched a few commands into the computer program, then paused as lines of text appeared on the computer screen before him. "This is most unusual. Why, Master Hoole, I seem to have stumbled upon—"

"Wait, Deevee," Hoole interrupted. He was studying a computer terminal that had hummed to life. "I believe I've found the security codes that open this door."

Hoole entered a series of numbers into the computer, and the inner door slid open with a loud rumble. Tash and Zak looked up as the door retracted to reveal a wide chamber with high ceilings. The walls were lined with electronic equipment. Hundreds of pipes and cables led to the center of the room, where they all connected to a single object. It was taller than Hoole, and made of gleaming black metal.

"It looks like an egg," said Tash.

"An electronic egg," added Zak.

"It's a birth chamber," Hoole said.

"A birth chamber," Zak repeated. "A birth chamber for what?"

Hoole studied the large egg-shaped chamber. The polished black metal hummed with power. "I do not know," he said quietly. He touched a control panel on the egg.

Nothing happened.

Hoole frowned. "He has changed the codes," the Shi'ido muttered. "I cannot open it."

Zak grinned. "I bet I can crack that egg."

He reached into his pack and pulled out the datadisks he had salvaged from the *Shroud*.

"What are you doing?" Tash asked.

"This is all the information that was in the *Shroud*'s computers. I've been studying it every chance I get. I haven't exactly broken its code, but I'm close. Well, maybe not close, but I know enough to know a list of computer codes when I see one. I'll bet the entry code is here somewhere. If I can just find the right disk . . ."

Sorting through the disks, Zak jabbed one into a slot in the egg's control panel. Nothing happened.

Zak grunted and tried another.

Deevee shook his head. "Zak, the odds of finding a single bit of information in dozens of datadisks and selecting it as an entry code are well over six hundred fifty thousand to—"

"Got it," Zak said.

There was a bleep as the egg's computer accepted the disk Zak had inserted. A screech of metal followed . . . and then the egg cracked. Tash and Zak stepped back as the top half of the egg titled backward and light poured from the chamber with an electronic hiss.

Something inside the egg moved.

Shielding their eyes from the bright light, Zak, Tash, and Hoole stepped forward and squinted into the birth chamber.

Inside the egg was a baby.

CHAPTER

Zak asked the question they were all thinking. "Hey, there. What are you doing in there, little guy?"

The baby, who looked almost a year old, gazed up from a round padded bed in the center of the egg and squealed in delight. He had on a tiny pair of coveralls, the kind that infant boys often wore. His eyes twinkled, and his toothless grin reached from ear to ear.

"He's beautiful," Tash said, leaning into the chamber.

"Don't touch it!" Hoole commanded.

Tash raised her eyebrow. "Why? He's just a little baby."

"You do not know what he is," the Shi'ido replied. "Not when he comes from Gog's laboratory."

"You're just a sweet little baby, aren't you?" Tash cooed at the little boy. "And silly old Uncle Hoole is a worry wampa, isn't he?"

"Eppon!" the baby yipped.

"What's that?" Zak asked.

"Eppon!" the baby gurgled.

"Is that your name?" Tash chuckled.

"Eppon!"

"Works for me," Zak laughed. "Nice to meet you, Eppon."

Tash ignored Hoole's protests and pulled the little boy out of the chamber. The baby crawled into her arms and clung to her with a happy smile on his face. "Eppon!"

Hoole glowered. "Tash, I suggest you put the child down immediately. We have no idea what that creature is."

Tash returned her uncle's glare. "Uncle Hoole, how can you be so cruel? We can't just leave this little boy sitting in the middle of nowhere. He's a helpless baby."

But before Hoole could respond, the doors behind them exploded open.

CHAPTER

Zak and Hoole threw their arms up to protect their faces. Tash hugged Eppon close to her.

Smoke billowed up from the blasted door. Seconds later, a squad of soldiers leaped through the open door, blasters burning the air with energy bolts. The Empire had found them!

Then Zak spotted one soldier much taller than the rest. The figure roared as it shook its shaggy head. It was a Wookiee.

"Chewbacca!" Zak called out.

The Wookiee roared again.

"Cease fire!" a woman's voice commanded. The firing stopped immediately.

Following the Wookiee, three other figures stepped out of

the smoke. There was a blond man, a darker man who moved with a confident swagger, and a beautiful young woman who had the clear eyes and proud bearing of a natural leader.

"Princess Leia!" Tash said excitedly. "Luke, Han! What are you doing here?"

Han Solo jammed his blaster back into its holster. "We could ask you the same question, kid. We haven't seen you since we all escaped from D'vouran."

Leia studied each of them, even Deevee, with a wry look on her face. "You four have a habit of showing up in the strangest places. I can only assume that this is no coincidence."

"As Han Solo said," Hoole replied, "we could say the same of you."

There were ten soldiers with the Rebel leaders, and Zak noticed the emblems on their uniforms. He recognized the Rebel symbol from smuggled news reports he'd seen on the HoloNet. "I knew it!" he said. "You guys *are* Rebels. I said so the minute we met you."

Hoole's dark eyes returned Leia's steady stare. "May I assume that you came here to learn more about Project Starscream?"

Leia was surprised, but only for a moment. "Actually, we came here to *destroy* Project Starscream. After D'vouran, we started investigating the Imperial Science Department and learned that the Empire was up to some-

37

thing—as they usually are. We finally learned the name Project Starscream and traced it to this planet.''

"Only to find that you'd gotten here first," Luke Skywalker said. He winked at Tash, and she felt the Force flow between them, just as she had during their first meeting. It was a warm, electric tingle, as though she were on one end of a wire with Luke at the other. Together, they made a connection. "I knew there was more to you than meets the eye," he said, looking at Tash.

Zak's eyes lit up. "Hey, it's a good thing you guys are here. You can give us a lift off planet. Our ship was blasted by an ion cannon and we crash-landed.''

Han jerked his thumb over his shoulder. "Yeah, we got fried by the same weapons. Our ships hit the surface pretty hard about fifty kilometers back, but the *Millennium Falcon* isn't too badly damaged. Thanks to my flying.''

Chewbacca barked something sarcastic. "Yeah, and Chewie's, too,'' Han translated. "Anyway, we left some technicians working on the problem. The ship'll be ready to fly by the time we get back there.''

"We can start just as soon as we make sure Project Starscream is destroyed,'' Leia said. "And, if possible, we'd like to question the being behind the project. Our sources tell us he's—''

"A Shi'ido named Borborygmus Gog,'' Hoole interrupted. "We know.''

Leia's eyes widened. She was obviously impressed.

Hoole continued. "But I'm afraid you won't be able to

38

question him. He died several days ago. I'm sure that any vital information died with him."

"Sounds like you've got quite a story to tell," Han said, shaking his head.

"Later," Leia said. "Right now, we should check to make sure Gog is gone. Threepio! Artoo!"

A golden, humanlike droid, very similar to Deevee in shape, shuffled forward, trailed by a squat, barrel-shaped companion. Tash and Zak recognized C-3PO and R2-D2.

"Here, Your Highness!" the golden droid, Threepio, called out. "We were just, er, guarding the rear."

Artoo emitted a series of whistles and squeaks.

"Be quiet, Artoo!" Threepio said. "You couldn't guard your servos from rust!"

Leia ignored them. "Artoo, plug into the main computer. I want to know everything there is to know about Project Starscream."

With a cheerful bleep, Artoo rolled over to the computer console and jammed his interface plug into an open socket.

Hoole explained. "I had been conducting my own investigation from a different angle. We encountered Gog before I knew that his headquarters were here on Kiva. When we got here, this facility was abandoned and there was nothing left of the project."

"Except him!" Tash laughed, lifting the little boy onto her shoulder. He had grabbed hold of her single neat braid of blond hair and was tugging at it. "We found him in that egg chamber."

"And just who are you, little one?" Leia said, holding the baby's chubby face in her hands.

"Eppon!" the boy squealed.

"We think that's his name," Tash explained. "It's the only word he knows."

Leia ran her finger through a thick layer of dust gathered on top of the computer console. "This place looks as though it's been deserted for some time. How could the baby have survived?"

Hoole pointed at the egg-shaped chamber. "I believe that's the purpose of this chamber. It was meant to keep the child alive during Gog's absence."

"This Gog, he must have been planning to experiment on the baby," Han said, sneering. "These Imperials are slimier than Jabba the Hutt."

"Well, he seems to have met his fate before he could do anything to this little one," Luke said, tickling the baby under the chin. Eppon giggled.

Artoo let out an excited bleep.

"Your Highness," Threepio explained. "Artoo says that he has downloaded this computer's files into his memory banks. If there ever were any files on Project Starscream, they've been destroyed."

"I knew it," Hoole said. "Gog was too careful to leave records lying about. Whatever he was planning, he has taken it to his grave."

"Well, let's make sure we don't take it to ours," Luke said. "I want to get off planet before trouble finds us."

"Relax," Han said with a yawn. "What trouble would find us in this deserted place?"

A few hours later, Zak and Tash were hiking through the rocks of Kiva once more. They had warned the Rebels about the strange shadow creatures, so the group kept a sharp lookout as they traveled. Behind the two Arrandas marched the squad of ten Rebel soldiers. Luke Skywalker walked with Tash and Zak, while Hoole strode in front, talking in low tones with Princess Leia and Han Solo. Before them all stalked the mighty Chewbacca, his sharp Wookiee senses scanning the landscape for trouble.

Zak, Tash, and Luke Skywalker took turns holding the baby. Eppon tugged at their hair and ran his hands over their faces as he giggled and cooed.

"I do not know how we will care for this child," Hoole mused. "We have no way to feed him, unless he can eat the supplies we brought from our ship."

"No need to worry about that right now," Luke responded. "All he's starved for is attention. It's like no one has ever held him or hugged him before."

"That's sad," Tash said. "Maybe he's an orphan."

"In that case, I know how he feels," Zak said.

"Me too," Luke Skywalker added quietly.

"Well, he's not an orphan anymore!" Tash perked up. "He's got *us*." She held the baby up in the air. "Eppon, from now on Zak and I are your brother and sister, and you are officially part of the Arranda family."

"Eppon!" the baby squealed happily.

Eppon squirmed so much that Tash almost dropped him. "Ugh, he's getting heavy. Zak, ready for another turn?"

Zak wiggled his arms like they were wet noodles. "Not me. My arms are about to fall off. Luke?"

The blond Rebel shrugged. "Sorry, kids. I've got to go up front with Chewie. Maybe one of the commandos will take a turn. Hey, Rax!"

One of the Rebel commandos hustled forward. "Yes, sir?"

"You mind doing some baby-sitting duty?"

The commando sighed. They could tell he didn't like the idea, but Luke was a hero of the Rebellion, so Rax slung his blaster rifle over his shoulder and pulled little Eppon up into his arms. Eppon buried his head in the soldier's neck. "Eppon!"

"He likes you!" Tash laughed.

"Hurray," the soldier groaned.

They marched on.

Soon they came to a field of rocks, standing like a small stone forest. There were tall, thin rocks that rose higher than Hoole's head, and shorter, thicker ones that only reached Tash's waist. Although stones like this covered the planet, here they grew so thick that one person could barely slip between them.

Han Solo called a halt. "We can't go through there and still watch each other's backs," he explained. "We'll have to scatter and get through as best we can."

42

"Maybe we should go around," Leia suggested.

"We'd lose a lot of time," Han replied. "Besides, I doubt there's anything to worry about."

"I shall make certain," Hoole said.

He closed his eyes. At first, he seemed to shiver as if he were cold. Then the skin crawled across his bones, and in the blink of an eye, he had changed shape . . . into a long, thin serpent. The serpent was nearly transparent, and difficult to see in Kiva's gray light.

Artoo bleeped.

"Quite right, Artoo," Threepio replied. "As a crystal snake, Master Hoole will have no trouble scouting out those rocks." Threepio lowered his voice. "I'm just glad he's going in that direction, and not toward me!"

The crystal snake slithered off through the stone field, slipping quickly through the openings. A few moments later they caught a glint of light on the far side. There was a blur of motion, and the snake changed back into Hoole. The tall Shi'ido waved his arms. The path was safe.

Leia waved back. "Okay, everyone, break formation. Let's hurry through."

The Rebel commandos broke ranks, and they all started to pick their way through the rocky forest. Since they were the smallest, Zak and Tash slipped easily through the maze of rocks, and quickly made it to the other side where Hoole waited. They watched as, one by one, the Rebels reached their side of the field. In a few moments they had all arrived, except . . .

43

"Where's Rax?" Han asked.

"Where's Eppon?" Tash asked.

"He was right behind me," one of the commandos said. "I thought he'd be—"

The Rebel didn't finish his sentence. A terrible scream ripped through the quiet air.

Everyone plunged back into the rock forest, running toward the direction of the scream. Zak and Tash were the first to arrive, followed closely by Hoole, Han Solo, and Luke Skywalker. What they found made them all gasp.

Lying on the ground was Eppon, curled up in a ball, sobbing. He looked like he had been dropped. Beside him lay Rax's blaster rifle, his clothes, his pack, and even his boots.

But the commando had vanished.

CHAPTER 7

Everyone burst into action at the same time. The Rebel commandos drew their weapons and immediately began searching the area. Zak and Tash ran to pick up Eppon, while Hoole and the Rebel leaders gathered around the remains of their companion.

"Poor baby," Tash said. "He's got a bruise on his arm."

"He's tough, though," Zak said. "He's already stopped crying."

Beside them, Leia touched the commando's crumpled clothes. They were completely empty. Leia scratched her head. "What do you think happened here?"

"I don't know," Han answered, "but Rax was a well-armed and well-trained commando. He wouldn't have gone down without a fight."

"It looks like Rax was pulled right out of his uniform.

Hoole, could it have been one of those shadow creatures you mentioned?'' Leia asked.

The Shi'ido shrugged. "I don't know. But they gave no indication that they had any such power.''

Luke Skywalker frowned. "I've got a bad feeling about this place.''

Chewie gave out a low, confused snarl, which Han translated. "Chewie says he doesn't smell anything. And there are no tracks. Whoever did this must be a ghost.''

Tash glanced at Hoole, and saw a look of sorrow cross his face.

Before she could comment, Han said gruffly, "Rax was a good man. Come on, let's get going. I want to make sure we don't lose anyone else on this little hike.''

The Rebels kept their weapons drawn as the group continued its march. But they heard and saw nothing.

"It's quiet,'' Tash whispered.

"As the grave,'' Zak agreed.

"Be silent,'' Hoole cautioned irritably.

Tash carried Eppon for a while; then, when they had marched about three kilometers from Gog's laboratory, she suddenly handed the baby boy over to Zak. "Will you hold him for a while?''

Zak pulled Eppon into his arms. "Sure . . . ugh! Is it me, or has he gotten heavier?''

"It's you, laser brain,'' his sister said. "You're just getting tired.''

"I'm not *that* tired. He's putting on weight!"

"Without eating anything?" Tash shook her head. "Do you think you can manage anyway? I want to go talk to Luke."

"We'll be all right, won't we, little guy?"

"Eppon!" the little boy chirped.

Tash hurried past Uncle Hoole, Han, and Leia, to where Luke Skywalker walked with Chewbacca at the front of the group. They were walking a dozen meters in front of the others, making sure there was nothing unpleasant awaiting the Rebel band. Tash caught up to them just as they were about to enter a narrow passage between two high rock walls.

"Luke, could I ask you a question?"

Luke turned back from studying the path between the two stone cliffs. "What is it, Tash?"

She hesitated. There were so many questions she wanted to ask, so much she wanted to know about the Jedi Knights and the Force. She had reason to believe that she could use the Force. But she didn't know how. And ever since her first meeting with Luke, she had guessed that he was a Jedi, or at least knew a lot about them. It wasn't just because he carried a lightsaber—she could feel it, like an energy field that surrounded him.

"How much—How much do you know about the Force?" she finally asked.

"Not much," Luke confessed. "Just what an old friend

told me. The Force is what gives a Jedi his power. It's a kind of energy field that binds the galaxy together. It connects all things.''

"Is it—Is it like a weapon?'' she continued.

Luke shook his head. "I don't think so. That's not the way to use the Force. Jedi Knights used it in battle, but the Force isn't a weapon like a blaster or a lightsaber. It's more like a power that helps you focus yourself and understand everything around you.''

Tash asked, "Can you use the Force?''

Luke shrugged modestly. "A little, I think. That's why I'm up here with Chewie. I don't have his sense of smell, but I sometimes get feelings. Kind of like an inner alarm.''

"Yeah!'' Tash said excitedly.

Luke raised an eyebrow. "Do you get that feeling?''

Now it was Tash's turn to shrug. "Well, I guess—''

Before she could answer, Chewie let out an ear-shattering roar. At the same time, Luke's eyes went wide with alarm, and he yelled, "Get down!'' He dropped to the rocks, pulling Tash down with him just as a blaster bolt screamed through the air overhead.

Chewbacca roared another warning, and Tash didn't need Han Solo to tell her what he was saying.

"Ambush!'' she repeated, as blaster bolts fell like an energy storm around them.

The Rebel company dove for cover among the rocks. One commando was too slow, and a blaster bolt struck his chest, spinning him around.

"Return fire!" Leia ordered. The air quickly grew hot from crisscrossing energy bolts.

"Who would be on a lifeless rock like this?" Han asked. "Pirates? Smugglers?"

"Worse," Leia said. "Look!"

On the path ahead of them, they could see figures slowly advancing. The figures were dressed in white armor, and white helmets masked their faces.

Stormtroopers.

"What's the Empire doing here?" Han complained.

"I don't know," Leia said. "But at least that answers our questions about Rax. The Imperials must have got him somehow."

"Why would they have left his clothes and equipment?" Luke asked, then ducked as a blaster bolt flashed overhead.

"Ask *them*!" Han shouted back. "All I want to know is how they found us."

"Maybe they tailed us," Luke called out from behind a rock.

"No way. No one followed me!" Han stated.

"I am afraid they may be after *us*," Hoole said. "We thought we had escaped some Imperial pursuers before we came here. Perhaps I can help. I can shape change into a creature that will—"

"I think that would be a very bad idea," Han said. "Look!"

They all looked up the path again. The stormtroopers scurried about, trying to remain hidden from Rebel blasters while they advanced. But one ominous figure stepped into the open and strode forward. His armor was as dark as his heart, and his cape swirled around him like a shadow.

"Darth Vader!" Leia shouted. "Fire!" she ordered.

The Rebels opened fire, pouring energy beams on the Dark Lord of the Sith. From his hiding place, Zak watched the blaster bolts streak toward Vader and figured that the Dark Lord was doomed. But Vader simply waved one gloved hand, and the blaster bolts changed course. They scattered like leaves blown by the wind.

"What the—?" Zak cried. "That's impossible!"

"We've got to stop him," Han growled.

"I've got an idea," Leia said. She raised her blaster, not at Vader, but at the rock wall above him, and fired. The blaster bolt struck the wall, blowing out a chunk of rock. More rocks followed it, and in moments a small avalanche of stones tumbled down onto the path right in front of Vader. When the dust settled, they saw that the falling rocks had blocked the path.

"Nice shooting, Leia!" Tash cheered.

"Not bad, Your Royalness," Han Solo admitted.

"It won't hold Vader back for long," Leia said. "We've got to do something."

"He must be after me," Luke said. "He's wanted revenge since we destroyed the Death Star."

"If that's true, then we should send Hoole, Zak, and Tash away," Leia said. "The ship should be repaired by now, and they'll be safer there. Vader won't bother them if he's after us.''

"We can't just leave you!" Tash argued.

"This is our fight, Tash," Luke said calmly. "Vader is more powerful than you can imagine. You've got to get out of here. We'll hold the Imperials off as long as we can."

Hoole shook his head. "We cannot allow you to risk your lives on our account."

"Hey, risking my life for other people's problems has become a hobby," Han smirked.

Leia pointed to four of the Rebel commandos. "Sikes! Bergan! Tino! Meex! Front and center!"

The four commandos hustled forward. "You guys have a new assignment. Get these civilians safely back to the ships. If we haven't joined you in four hours, blast off this planet and don't look back."

"Yes, Your Highness!" said the commandos.

"We're leaving," Hoole said. "Where's the child?"

"I hid him over here where it was safe from the blaster fire," Zak said. "He's right behind this rock."

Zak stepped behind the rock, and gasped.

The baby was now a little boy.

CHAPTER

8

"I cannot claim to be an expert," said Deevee, "but I believe this rate of growth is impossible for human children."

"A little while ago he was about a year old," Zak said. "Now he looks like he could be three."

"Eppon!" the little boy squeaked.

"No time to worry about it," the commando named Meex said. "I'll carry him." He scooped the boy up easily and the small party started off.

In order to put distance between them and the Imperials, they doubled back until they reached the field of stones. There, they turned left, and started to pick a new trail back over the tough, rocky terrain of Kiva. The commandos thought they could still reach the ships in an hour or two.

Tash and Zak looked back a few times as they hurried

away from the battlefield. The Imperials must have broken through the avalanche, because blaster fire had started up again.

"I hope they're all right," Tash whispered.

"I'm sure they will be," Hoole said. "As for us, we've done what we came here to do. Gog's headquarters are abandoned. Now we must get off this planet as soon as possible."

"You don't suppose we're in any more danger, do you, Master Hoole?" Deevee worried. "After all, I assume it was the Imperials who were responsible for the disappearance of that first commando."

"Perhaps," Hoole said. "But there are other dangers."

The Shi'ido pointed to a large gully on their right. At first Tash didn't see anything. Then she realized that the gully was full of shadows. And the shadows were moving.

"Wraiths," she whispered.

"Indeed," Hoole said coldly. "They have been following us since we left the abandoned laboratory."

Tash was surprised. "And you didn't say anything?"

Hoole didn't answer.

The Rebel commandos had spotted the strange shadows, too. They picked up the pace. "Our landing point is only a few more kilometers from here," said Meex. "If we hurry, we can—"

"They're attacking!" one of the other commandos cried.

The shadows closed in. They did so slowly and steadily, moving just like a shadow growing longer in the afternoon.

53

The small group tried to look for a way to escape, but every path was blocked by darkness.

The shadows began to wail.

Murderer!

Mammon!

Killer!

Mammon!

KillerkillerkillerkillerkillerkillerKILLER!

One of the shadows seemed to rise off the ground. It reared up like a figure made of solid darkness, and lunged forward.

The commandos fired their weapons, and the blaster bolts shrieked into the dark curtain. The whispering turned to angry snarls, but nothing else happened.

"Blasters are useless," said Meex. "Try thermal detonators."

Another commando pulled a fist-sized metal ball from his belt and tossed it into the darkness. "Everybody down!"

They all crouched and shielded their eyes as the grenade exploded. Brilliant white light flashed around them for a moment, driving the shadows away. But the shadows came back as the light faded, and came toward them again.

The Rebel commandos made a small circle with Hoole, Deevee, Zak, and Tash squeezed into the middle. Only a few meters of light separated them from the wraiths. Tash could see the wraiths in their own darkness, angry figures writhing about, gathering themselves to attack. And she could feel them, too. They were angry. She sensed that anger was all they had left. It was the only part of them that was still alive.

Murderer! Murderer!

The commandos fired several more shots into the shadows, but it was no use.

"Uncle Hoole, what should we do?" Zak asked.

Hoole didn't answer. He stood stone still, staring into the darkness. His eyes seemed very far away. He seemed to be waiting.

Tash turned to Meex. "What should we do?"

The commando shook his head. "Blasters don't work. Grenades don't work. I sure don't want to fight these things hand to hand, whatever they are."

"Do you have any ion weapons?" Zak asked.

Meex raised an eyebrow. "Well, yeah, we've got a portable ion gun. It's used to fight off attacking airships. But ion weapons don't do any good against living creatures."

Zak nodded. "It will against these. Hurry!"

"Bergan!" Meex snapped. "Tino! Assemble the ion gun. On the double!"

The two commandos pulled open their packs and dumped out several large pieces of equipment. In a few seconds, they had snapped the pieces together to form a small cannon mounted on legs.

"Seems like a waste of time," Meex said. "But here goes. Fire!"

The commandos pointed their ion cannon at the shadows

and fired. White bolts of energy punched the gathered wraiths. Then screams burst from the darkness, and the shadows parted.

"That's done it!" Meex cheered. "Fire at will!"

The cannon fired again and again. The shadows fled screaming in terror, but the commandos kept firing.

To everyone's surprise, Hoole suddenly snapped out of his trance. He bellowed, "Stop! Stop your firing! Do not harm them! Stop!"

The Rebels were trained to follow orders, but not Hoole's orders, so they kept firing.

The wraiths scattered and vanished among the rocks, but the Rebels trained the ion cannon on one of the fleeing creatures and poured fire on it. The wraith shrieked and fell. It lay there like a pool of dark liquid collecting on the rocky ground.

"Got one!" the Rebels cried.

"No!" Hoole moaned.

Cautiously, the group approached the fallen wraith. It was a strange sight to see, a shadow curled up on the ground. Zak kept expecting to see someone standing nearby, a person to cast the shadow, but there was nothing. Just the shadow.

These creatures must be made of energy, Zak thought. *That's why the ion cannon affects them.*

The wraith stirred.

"Watch it!" Meex ordered. "It could still be dangerous."

56

"I don't think so," Tash replied.

Writhing and squirming like boiling water, the wraith formed itself into a humanoid shape. They could see the outline of two arms, shoulders, and a head. Out of the head came a weak, fading voice.

Murderer.

Tash was the first to speak. "Why did you attack us? Why do you call us 'murderer'?"

Killer, the wraith snarled. *We seek revenge!*

"Revenge?" Zak replied. "Why on us?"

We demand justice! We must avenge ourselves on the one who destroyed all life on our planet. The one who turned us into shadow creatures! We will kill you!

Tash pointed to herself and her companions. "But you've got it wrong. We didn't harm your people."

Not you, the wraith whispered, stabbing one shadowy arm forward. *Him!*

The wraith pointed directly at Uncle Hoole.

CHAPTER

The silence that followed the wraith's words was terrible.

Tash thought she could hear her own heart pounding in her chest. Beside her, Zak tried to steady himself so that he wouldn't fall over.

What did it mean?

Hoole stood with his eyes downcast. His face was as sad and gray as the sky above them.

Finally, Zak spoke. He looked at the shadow creature. ''Th-There's got to be a mistake.''

The wraith's voice had faded even more. *No. He is the killer. He destroyed my people.*

''Uncle Hoole,'' Tash pleaded, ''tell him he's wrong. Tell him there's been a mistake.''

The frown on Hoole's face deepened. Suddenly, he looked very old, and very, very tired. He opened his mouth to speak, but at that moment, the wraith let out an angry hiss. A moment later the wraith itself vanished. All that was left was a cold, dark stain on the rocky ground.

Hoole closed his mouth without speaking. Then he did the last thing Zak and Tash expected.

He turned and walked away.

"Uncle Hoole?" Zak called out in surprise.

Hoole did not turn around. Stunned, they watched him go. In a few seconds, he had disappeared among the rocks.

"Deevee," Tash asked the droid, "where's he going? Should we follow him?"

The silver droid slowly shook his mechanical head. "I do not know, Tash. I truly do not know."

The commando Meex finally spoke. "Wherever he's going, it's a security breach. My orders are to get you to the ships, and that's what I'm gonna do. Tino and Bergan, you stay with the equipment and the ion cannon. Watch the kid, Sikes. The rest of you, you're with me."

"We should stay with Eppon," Tash said.

"No, I may need you to help me find your uncle," Meex ordered.

"What about the wraiths?" Deevee asked.

Meex grimaced. "Sounds like those creatures are after Hoole, not us. We won't have to worry about them unless we find him. Which is what we're going to do right now. Let's go!"

But Meex was wrong. They did not find Hoole, even though Zak, Tash, and Deevee helped search. After half an hour of looking and finding nothing, they decided to give up.

Meex agreed. "Tough to find someone who doesn't want to be found."

"Especially when that someone's a Shi'ido," Zak added, kicking a rock in frustration. "He could shapeshift into a rock mouse and hide from us. We'd never find him."

"What's wrong with him?" Tash asked Deevee. "He's been acting strange ever since we arrived here. Why didn't he help us the first time the wraiths attacked?"

"And why didn't he want the commandos to shoot them?" Zak added.

"And why didn't he explain to the wraiths that they had made some sort of mistake?" Tash finished. "Do you think . . ." She swallowed. "Do you think Uncle Hoole really could be responsible?"

Zak shook his head. "No way. There's got to be a mistake."

Deevee paused. "I may know the answers. But it will take some time to explain."

"Then it'll have to wait," Meex insisted. "We'll go back and get my men and the kid, then start marching again. You can tell your story when we're safe."

As they hurried back to find the others, Tash was filled with a growing sense of fear. It was like a knot tightening in her stomach. She knew what it meant.

"We've got to hurry," she said as they all stumbled through the rocky terrain. "We're in danger."

"I—I think I know what you mean," Zak said. "I've got a really bad feeling about this place."

For a few seconds, the air of Kiva was filled with the sounds of their running feet. Then another sound broke through the silence. It was the sound of terrified human voices calling out in the distance.

"No! Help!" the voices cried.

"That's Bergan and Tino!" Meex yelled.

A single blaster shot echoed through the air, followed by more cries. "No! *Ahhhh!*"

Then the silence fell again.

"Come on!"

They found what was left of all three commandos. Bergan's, Tino's, and Sikes's clothes and equipment lay in a pile, as though their bodies had vanished into thin air.

"No sign of struggle, no blood, no nothing," Meex growled. "What is going on here?"

"Where's Eppon?" Tash asked, panicked.

"Eppon!" came a small peep.

The little boy had crawled into a dry riverbed near them. He giggled and toddled toward Tash, who picked him up. "I'm glad you're all right, little one," she whispered.

"How'd he get in there?" Zak asked. "Not too long ago he could barely crawl."

"Perhaps one of the soldiers tossed him in there when the wraiths attacked," Deevee suggested. "That's how the boy escaped injury."

"He didn't totally escape," Tash noted. "Look at this."

There was a purple bruise the size of a bird's egg on Eppon's forehead. It had already swelled up. "Poor Eppon," Tash cooed.

"Eppon!" the baby echoed.

"We've got to get out of here," Meex stated.

Tash bristled. "Not without Uncle Hoole."

Meex was about to reply sharply, when Zak stepped between them. "Tash, with the ship's onboard sensors, we could scan the entire planet for Hoole. It would be faster."

Tash wasn't sure, but replied, "Well, if you say so, Zak."

Deevee offered to carry Eppon on his back. Using strips of cloth from Sikes's uniform, they rigged a crude sack, placed Eppon in it, and slung the bag over Deevee's metallic shoulders.

"Ready?" Tash asked.

"I should think so," Deevee replied. "I'd like to reach safety before it gets dark."

Tash looked up at the sky. It was the same dull gray they'd seen when they first arrived. "The light hasn't changed. I don't think it's ever nighttime here. It's always twilight."

Meex packed up the ion cannon and prepared to move. "Double time," Meex ordered. "Let's go!"

At first Zak and Tash had no trouble keeping up with the pace the commando set. But soon their breath started to come short, and their feet started to feel as heavy as planets. Zak was ready to collapse at any moment. Deevee suddenly let out a cry of alarm and stumbled to his knees with a crash of metal arms and legs. The makeshift sack holding Eppon flew off his shoulders and landed in a heap beside him.

"By the Maker!" said the droid. "I think I've dented myself. And so soon after being repaired!"

"You dropped Eppon!" Tash scolded, running over to the pile of rags.

Zak helped the droid get to his feet. "What happened, Deevee?"

"I don't know, Zak," the droid replied. "I was hurrying along when suddenly my balance gyros malfunctioned. I can't imagine why."

"I can," Tash said. "Look!"

She had pulled the rags and knots from around little Eppon. Except that he wasn't very little anymore. He had grown larger, and now looked about four or five years old. He had sleek black hair that reached down to his shoulders and very dark eyes. His skin was smooth and pale, except where the ugly bruise, which had gotten bigger, covered his forehead.

"This isn't natural," Meex said suspiciously.

"I must agree with you," Deevee said. "Obviously, we did not rescue this child before Gog began his experiments. Something has been done to the poor boy."

Meex took a step forward. "I hate to say it, but maybe that kid is more trouble than he's worth."

Tash pulled Eppon closer to her. He was now almost too

63

heavy to lift, but she hugged him tight. "No! There are obviously plenty more dangerous things in this place."

Zak came to his sister's defense. "So what do you want to do, just leave Eppon out here? Let him die of thirst? Look at him! He's still just a kid." Zak looked into Eppon's eyes. "Eppon, can you talk? Can you say anything? Is your brain growing just like your body?"

For an answer, Eppon simply smiled as sweetly as a newborn baby and laughed. He hugged Tash. "Eppon!"

Meex's face softened, and Zak and Tash could tell they'd won the argument.

Eppon had grown out of the tiny coverall he'd been dressed in. Meex grudgingly pulled a tunic out of his pack. It was far too large for Eppon, but they rolled up the sleeves, and tied it around the waist with a length of cord. It looked like an enormous robe, but it did the job, and they started off again.

They hurried on under a dark cloud. Tash and Zak were concerned about Uncle Hoole. They were all worried about who might vanish next. Only Eppon seemed unaffected. He still could not speak, but he laughed and skipped along beside Tash, croaking "Eppon!" at anything that interested him.

Their gloom lifted slightly as they scrambled up a rocky hill and saw, on the far side, two starships nestled in a dry, dusty field. One of the vessels was a simple cargo ship. The other was shaped like a saucer, and looked like it had been strung together with glue and good luck. But those who recognized it knew that it was one of the fastest ships in the galaxy.

"The *Millennium Falcon*," Zak said admiringly.

"Safety!" Deevee sighed. "At last."

Meex nodded. "Let's hope the technicians have made all the repairs."

They ran down the slope and hurried to the ships. Meex called out, but there was no reply. They checked the *Millennium Falcon*. No one was aboard.

Tash shuddered, thinking of the wraiths. "Do you suppose—?"

"You stay here," Meex ordered. "I'm going to check out the other ship."

"I don't think that's a good idea," Zak argued. "We should stick together. Maybe we could fly one of these ships to get the others, and then scan for Uncle Hoole."

"Not until I find out what happened to the crew we left here," Meex said. He looked suspiciously at Eppon. "If the wraiths got them, I want proof."

Through the *Falcon*'s cockpit window, Tash, Zak, and Deevee watched Meex creep slowly to the other ship, moving quietly, his weapon drawn. Meex reached the ship and pressed himself against the hull, holding his blaster steady. Then he opened the hatch, and quickly jabbed his blaster inside.

Nothing happened.

Cautiously, he slipped inside the cargo ship.

Tash and Zak waited for three minutes. Five minutes. Seven minutes.

When ten minutes had passed, Tash whispered, "It seems like we've been waiting forever. Should we go after him?"

Zak shook his head. "Not yet."

Eppon's eyes were riveted on the other ship. "Eppon," he whispered.

"What if he doesn't come back?" Tash wondered aloud.

"At least we're safe for the moment," said Deevee.

"Eppon!" Eppon suddenly shouted. Before they could stop him, he scampered out of the cockpit and toward the exit.

"Stop!" Tash and Zak yelled, starting after him.

"Wait!" Deevee called out.

Tash and Zak were faster, and they reached the hatch ahead of the droid. They dashed outside to see Eppon streaking toward the other ship. They were both surprised at his speed—hours ago Eppon couldn't even walk. Now he was running faster than any five-year-old possibly could.

"Eppon, stop!" the two Arrandas yelled.

They were so busy watching the boy, they did not notice the shadows creeping toward them.

"What's he doing?" Tash gasped to Zak.

"What makes you think I know?" Zak retorted. "I can't even see him anymore. He ran into the shadow of the ship."

Zak pulled up short, his heart suddenly leaping into his throat.

The shadow of the starship had suddenly grown enormous.

And it was still growing.

In seconds, the giant shadow had surrounded them.

"Oh, no."

That was all Zak had time to whisper before a great wave of darkness rose up and fell crashing down around them, and everything went black.

CHAPTER

Zak had no idea why he had passed out, or how much time had gone by since he did. All he knew when he awoke was that his arms and legs felt heavy, like he was waking from a deep sleep. The back of his head was sore—he felt like he'd been using a rock for a pillow. His eyes were closed, and it was very dark. He opened his eyes.

The darkness didn't go away.

Zak blinked to make sure his eyes were really open. The darkness around him was complete. It was darker than a deep hole, darker than deep space itself.

''Where am I?'' he said aloud.

A thousand whispering voices answered him at the same time. *You are in the heart of our misery! You are at the center of our hatred!*

Zak felt the wraiths moving all around him. When they

brushed over his skin, it felt like a sudden gust of warm, musty air. Zak knew that the wraiths could tear him to shreds at any moment. He shuddered.

His hand touched something soft beside him. It was cloth. Groping about, he felt Tash's hand. He found her shoulder and shook it gently. "Tash. Tash!"

Although she was less than an arm's length away, he could not see her, but he heard her stir. "Zak?" she muttered drowsily. "Zak, where are we?" Then, her voice trembling, she said, "Oh, no. The wraiths."

Zak nodded. "They've got us."

Zak and Tash stood up together, holding hands. They felt stone beneath their feet, and knew that they were standing somewhere on Kiva. But everywhere they looked, they could see nothing but darkness.

"What do we do now?" Zak wondered.

"I don't know," Tash replied from the darkness. "We've lost Uncle Hoole. We've lost Deevee. Meex is gone. Eppon ran away. We're—We're alone again."

Zak squeezed her hand. "Not while we've got each other." His voice hardened. "Maybe we can fight our way out of here."

"No, we shouldn't fight them, Zak," Tash said firmly. "Whatever these creatures are, they're angry, they're full of pain. Something terrible happened to them, and for some reason they blame us. We've got to make them understand that we don't mean any harm."

Zak felt a wraith pass close by, its shadowy form brushing the back of his neck with a hiss. He shivered. "I'll try anything."

Tash called out, "We haven't done anything to you. We're not your enemy!"

Murderers! Children of the murderer! a thousand voices replied. *Listen to us! Once, a beautiful civilization thrived on Kiva. Now nothing is left but our tortured spirits.*

"Maybe we can help," Tash offered.

Her words caused a violent hiss to crisscross the darkness. When it stopped, the voices mocked, *Help? Help? Years ago, strangers came to Kiva offering help. They promised to make us great and powerful. Instead, they destroyed us! All our people were wiped out! They disintegrated our bodies, leaving only our shadows.*

"We're sorry!" Zak yelled. "We know how terrible that must have been."

You cannot know! the shadows wailed. *Have you ever lost your whole world?*

"Yes, we have!" Tash cried out. "The Empire destroyed our homeworld, Alderaan. We lost everything!"

Her words caused a strange reaction. The darkness seemed to swirl about itself, suddenly confused. The wraiths whispered among themselves. Finally, one voice spoke above the others.

But you came here with the murderer! You are the children of Mammon!

"No, we're not!" Zak said. "We didn't come here with any murderer. Who are you talking about?"

"They are talking," replied another voice out of the darkness, "about me."

The darkness parted like a curtain, and into the center of the black circle stepped a solitary figure with slumped shoulders and a tortured look on his face.

It was Uncle Hoole.

CHAPTER

The wraiths closed around Hoole, leaving him and the Arrandas in the dark.

Murderer! Killer! Revenge! Revenge! the voices chanted.

"Uncle Hoole?" Tash asked, reaching out to him. She found her uncle's hand and held it. "What do they mean? What's going on here?"

"It's time you knew the truth about me." Hoole's voice drifted from the darkness. The strong, commanding tone Zak and Tash were used to was gone. In its place was a quiet whisper, telling them a sad story.

"Zak, you once pointed out that I had never told you and Tash my name. I was Hoole, and that was all you needed to know. The truth is that I abandoned my first name years ago. I tried to leave it buried in the past."

There was a pause.

"My first name is Mammon."

The shadows hissed.

Hoole continued. "Almost twenty years ago I was a scientist. I thought I was brilliant, and I wanted to become famous in the field of genetics. I didn't want to just clone things. I wanted to create life.

"When the Emperor came to power, I saw my opportunity. The Empire encouraged research in new areas of science. Another scientist and I were given millions of credits by the Empire and allowed to begin our experiments."

"You worked for the Empire?" Tash said, hardly believing it. "Didn't you know how evil the Empire was?"

"No," Hoole replied. "No one knew how evil the Emperor was until it was too late. Besides, I was too busy with my research. Eventually, we finished our basic experiments. We needed more room, a larger facility. To create life out of nothing, we learned, we would need an incredible amount of energy. The Emperor built a huge laboratory here, on Kiva. Here, we explored the secrets of life itself."

Hoole took a deep breath before continuing his story, as the wraiths continued to hiss and swarm around them.

"We created huge generators that could focus the power of an entire star into one tiny test tube. But we lost control of our experiments. Instead of creating new life, we let loose a blast of energy that swept across the entire planet, wiping out every living thing."

"And then you just left these wraiths to suffer?" Zak asked.

Hoole shook his head. "No. I had no idea that the Kivans survived at all. The accident . . . it happened so fast. I tried to broadcast a warning, but the energy we released disrupted the transmission. My partner and I barely escaped before the explosion."

A terrible thought snaked its way into Tash's mind. She tried to hold it back, but it was too strong, too terrible. Several old, nagging questions repeated themselves in her brain.

How had Hoole known about Project Starscream and its leader?

How did so many underworld figures like Boba Fett and Jabba the Hutt know Hoole?

How did Hoole know where Gog's headquarters would be?

Finally, she asked the question, afraid of hearing the answer. "Who was your partner? Who was the other scientist?"

Hoole's voice was filled with agony. "It was Gog."

"No," Tash said.

"That's impossible," Zak said. "This is all some kind of terrible lie. It can't be true. Gog nearly killed us, and you *worked* with him?" His voice became shrill with anger.

"Zak, Tash, there's more to the story—"

"I don't care!" Tash said, her voice cracking. "You lied to us. And what's worse," she choked, "you destroyed an entire planet. All these creatures—you turned them into nothing but ghosts. What you did . . . it was as bad as what the Empire did to Alderaan!''

"All that you say," said Hoole, "is true."

Zak broke in, his voice full of bitterness. "I'll bet that's why you wanted to take care of us. When Alderaan was destroyed, it reminded you of your own crime. You felt guilty. You didn't take us in because you cared about us. You just wanted to make yourself feel better!''

Hoole said nothing.

The shadows closed in. The wraiths pressed about them so thickly that they became almost solid.

The voices declared, *Years ago we swore vengeance. Today we shall have it. The murderer Mammon will be punished for his crimes.*

"What are you going to do to him?" Zak asked.

Before we were destroyed, our laws stated that victims had the right to confront those who harmed them. Thousands upon thousands died here because of him. He will stand here, and be forced to hear the agonized voices of each person he destroyed.

Tash and Zak both shuddered.

The voices continued. *And then, when Mammon has seen all the misery he has caused, he will be executed!*

CHAPTER 12

He will be executed!

The phrase was repeated over and over again, carried through the shadows by hundreds and thousands of voices.

Hoole remained as still as stone.

Tash and Zak felt shadowy hands grab them. They were pushed from behind and pulled from the front, carried away from Hoole. Seconds later, the shadows parted, and Tash and Zak found themselves standing in the gray light of Kiva once again, not far from where the *Millennium Falcon* had landed.

Turning quickly around, they saw, in the center of the valley, a huge, quivering shadow-dome like the one they'd seen earlier. Only this time they were on the outside.

For a moment, the two Arrandas just stood there, dazed. Neither of them knew exactly how to feel. Hoole had taken them in, he had cared for them. He had even saved their lives, more than once. But he had also kept a terrible secret from them.

Zak was the first to speak. "I can't believe it."

"He lied to us," Tash said.

"He—He's a murderer."

"Worse than a murderer," Tash said. "A planet-killer." She paused. "But he's still our uncle."

Zak nodded. "He's done so much for us. And he's still in there. They're going to kill him! What do we do?"

Tash shook her head. "He didn't seem to want to be saved. And I'm not sure we could save him. Maybe we should go back to the ships to find Deevee and Eppon. Then figure out what to do."

Zak felt numb. "We can't just leave him in there."

"What choice do we have?" his sister replied.

Zak had no answer.

Together, they started back toward the *Millennium Falcon*. Neither of them spoke. Neither of them wanted to admit the horrible truth going through both their minds: they weren't sure they *wanted* to save Hoole.

They reached the *Falcon* and the cargo ship. As they approached, two figures hurried toward them. One shone silvery in the gray light. The other looked like Eppon except . . .

"He's bigger!" Zak groaned.

"It appears to be true," Deevee agreed. "I found the boy again only a few minutes after you vanished. He had already grown to this size. Fortunately, I was able to locate a spare jumpsuit in the cargo ship. It fits him rather well.''

Zak stood next to the mysterious boy. ''I'll say. He's bigger than me.''

It was true. Eppon had grown into a teenage boy. His hair now reached well past his shoulders. His face had lost all its baby fat, and he had started to develop strong muscles in his arms. Even his voice had changed.

''Eppon!'' he said in a deep-throated bark.

''That mark is bigger, too,'' Tash noticed. The purple bruise on his brow had spread. It covered most of his forehead now and looked like it was spreading down his face. ''It looks bad. What do you think it is, Deevee?''

Deevee shook his head. ''My knowledge of biology is limited. Also, based on his rapid rate of growth, I would say this boy is not entirely human, so I cannot say for sure what illness he might have.''

The only thing that hadn't changed about Eppon was the twinkle in his eye for Zak and Tash. He smiled at them both and said again, ''Eppon!''

Deevee was equally delighted to see them. ''I thought I'd never see you two again! What happened?''

They hurried into the *Falcon* as Zak and Tash explained how the wraiths had captured them. When they got to the part about Hoole's confession, Deevee did not seem surprised. ''I must confess that I had my suspicions,'' the droid said.

Zak's eyes went wide. ''What? How long have you—?''

"Not long," the droid explained. "In fact, I had no idea until a few hours ago. It was the droid Artoo-Detoo who told me. Do you recall how he plugged into the fortress computer?"

"Yes," Tash said. "He said he couldn't find any files about Project Starscream."

Deevee nodded. "That is true. But he did find some old files from twenty years ago. They revealed that two Shi'ido had been running the experiments that destroyed Kiva. After that, I put my highly efficient computer brain to work. However, I wasn't completely sure until you told your story."

Tash shook her head. "All this time. We were with him all this time, and we never knew that he had done such a terrible thing."

Deevee's photoreceptors focused on her. "You should know that there's more to the story than that. In fact, Master Hoole—"

Deevee was interrupted by an ear-shattering screech of static. The *Falcon*'s comm system had suddenly activated. After a few seconds of electronic scratching, a voice poured through the speakers.

"Anybody there? Come in, somebody. Anyone copy?"

Zak recognized the voice. "That's Han Solo!" He rushed to the control panel and flipped a switch.

"We read you, Han."

There was a pause. "Is that you, kid? Let me talk to one of the commandos."

"They're all gone!" Tash yelled over her brother's shoulder. "We're the only ones left."

They heard Han swear on the other end of the transmission. Then he said, "Look, you have to get out of there. The Imperials are headed right for you!"

"But why?" Deevee wondered. "I thought they were after Master Skywalker."

"So did we," Han said through the speakers. "We tried to lead them away, but the minute Vader realized you weren't with us, he broke off the attack and headed for the ships. It looks like he's after you!"

Cold panic gripped Zak and Tash. Darth Vader was after them.

"What do you think we should do?" Tash asked hoarsely.

"Your only chance is to fly out of there," Han said.

"All right!" Zak cheered, eagerly scanning the *Falcon*'s control board.

"But don't take the *Falcon,*" Han added. "You'd never be able to fly her. Go over to the cargo ship. I'll contact you there and tell you how to start the engines."

"Blaster bolts," Zak spat. "I could so fly it."

"Copy. *Falcon* out," Tash replied.

She led her brother, Deevee, and Eppon out of the *Falcon* and over to the other ship. Remembering how Meex had disappeared inside the ship and never come out again, they entered cautiously. But they saw nothing. The ship was empty. They hurried to the cockpit, where Han Solo's voice was already filtering out of the speakers.

"We're here, Han," Tash said.

The speakers crackled. "Great. Here's what you do—"

They never heard his instructions. A blaster bolt flashed over their shoulders and smashed into the control board, sending a shower of sparks into the air.

Tash, Zak, and Deevee whirled around, expecting to see Imperial stormtroopers behind them.

Instead they saw a face from beyond the grave.

The face of a Shi'ido.

The face of Borborygmus Gog.

"You're dead!" Zak blurted out.

Gog grinned an evil grin. His clothes were torn and stained with oil and dirt. His face was covered in scratches and bruises. He was a Shi'ido like Hoole, and the first time she had seen Gog, Tash had mistaken him for her uncle. But any resemblance was now long gone.

"You're dead!" Zak repeated numbly. "We saw you fall into a pit."

The evil scientist shook his head. "You should have looked more closely. I did not die." Gog's eyes burned like lasers. "But if I had died, I would have come back from the grave just to get my revenge on you two interfering brats!"

Angrily, Gog let loose another blaster bolt. This one sizzled past Zak's cheek, destroying the ship's viewscreen behind him. The two Arrandas, Deevee, and Eppon cringed as a shower of sparks rose into the air.

"This has got to be some kind of nightmare," Tash moaned.

Deevee said, "I would agree with you, if I were capable of nightmares, Tash. How could Gog have followed us here?"

That seemed to make the Shi'ido even angrier. "Followed *you* here? Followed *you* here?" he said in a shrill voice. "It is you who followed *me* here. You and your pathetic uncle have dogged my steps from experiment to experiment, ruining every stage of Project Starscream. And when I come back to my own home, to save the last of my precious plans, what do I find? You have taken that, too! It took me twenty years of work to develop my ultimate weapon, and you have stolen it!"

Tash raised her eyebrows. Gog was ranting like a madman. "When we got to your lab, it was deserted," she said. "We didn't take anything."

Gog's face went blank for a moment. Then he started to chuckle. The chuckle turned into a roaring laugh as his eyes burned into them. "Ha! You mean you don't know? You haven't realized yet? Then you are greater fools than I ever dreamed!" He jabbed one long, bony finger at them. "You had the ultimate weapon in your hands and never knew it!"

Zak and Tash realized that he wasn't pointing at them. He was pointing at Eppon.

"Come here!" Gog ordered.

Eppon took a step forward, then hesitated. He smiled at Zak and Tash, and started toward them.

"No!" Gog snapped. "I said *here*! Obey!"

At Gog's second command Eppon hurried obediently to the scientist's side. He crouched down at Gog's feet, and the Shi'ido put one hand on the boy's head as if he were a tame pet.

Zak and Tash were stunned. "What have you done to him?"

Gog laughed again. "Done to him? Done to him? I *made* him. He is my creation. He is the result of all my years of work. He is my ultimate weapon!"

"Eppon!" the boy repeated.

Eppon.

Weapon.

Zak and Tash exchanged a horrified glance. They realized that the little boy had only been repeating the one word Gog had used to describe him.

"You nearly ruined everything," Gog growled to Zak, Tash, and Deevee. "You let my living planet loose, you toppled my experiments with the undead. You destroyed my virus experiments and my Nightmare Machine. At Nespis 8 you used that accursed Force, the one power I cannot control, to defeat me. But I still have my ultimate weapon."

"What is he?" Tash asked, horrified.

"He and others like him will help me conquer the galaxy. He is the first soldier in my Army of Terror."

Tash looked worriedly at Eppon. "Why does he grow so quickly?"

Gog leered as he leveled his blaster. "You'll never know."

Zak and Tash looked around desperately, but there was nowhere to hide, no way to escape. They tensed, waiting for the shots that would end their lives. A second later, the sound of a blaster shot ripped through the air.

But it came from outside the ship.

It was followed by another, and another. Soon a storm of blaster bolts was pounding the cargo ship, making it shake on its landing gear.

"Look!" Deevee pointed out the transparisteel viewport.

Dozens of Imperial stormtroopers were closing in on the ship. Amid the crowds of white armor, the tall, dark figure of Darth Vader stood out.

"No!" Gog yelled. "No, no, no!"

The Shi'ido dashed toward the exit hatch with Eppon close behind him. Zak, Tash, and Deevee looked at each other blankly.

"He's as frightened of Vader as we are," Zak guessed.

"That makes no sense," Deevee observed. "They are all Imperials."

"I guess that doesn't necessarily make them friends," Tash said.

They crept toward the exit hatch and found it open. Peeking around the edge, they looked outside.

Gog was standing beside the ship, with Eppon squatting

beside him. Darth Vader stood a few meters away, a squad of stormtroopers at his back.

Vader's deep, rasping voice boomed across the distance between them. "Give me the boy."

"He's mine!" Gog protested. "The Emperor put *me* in charge of Project Starscream! He is my weapon."

Zak whispered, "It looks like Han was only part right. Vader wasn't after the Rebels, but he wasn't really after us, either. He wants Eppon!"

"Poor Eppon," Tash said. "He's just a tool they're fighting over."

Vader took a menacing step toward the Shi'ido. "He belongs to the Emperor. Give him to me."

"Never!"

Vader raised a gloved fist. Gog started to choke, clawing helplessly at his throat. The Dark Lord intoned, "You are fortunate that the Emperor wants you alive, Gog. Otherwise, I would make you feel the true power of the Force."

Vader dropped his hand, and Gog collapsed, gulping air.

"Take them both," Vader ordered.

The stormtroopers rushed forward.

"Looks like Gog finally met his match," Zak whispered.

"At least he'll never bother us again," Deevee sighed.

Tash's eyes went wide. "Don't be so sure!"

Still holding his half-crushed throat, Gog had managed to get to his knees. He pointed at Eppon and, in a rasping voice, wheezed, "Defend me! Defend me!"

Instantly, Eppon sprang at the advancing troopers. For a

split second, the two humans and the droid wondered what one unarmed teenage-sized boy could do against the Emperor's toughest soldiers. In the next second, their question was answered.

Eppon jumped on the nearest trooper and ripped his helmet off, exposing the soldier's startled face. The moment Eppon's hands touched the trooper's skin, the soldier screamed. What happened next was so unbelievable, so horrifying, that even the battle-hardened stormtroopers cried out in terror.

The stormtrooper's face turned to jelly. Then, with a loud, wet slurping sound, Eppon sucked the liquefied skin into himself. He simply absorbed the trooper's face into his own body.

The rest of the stormtrooper quickly followed. Skin, bone, organs, everything, simply turned to liquid and was absorbed into Eppon.

Tash and Zak both gagged.

The trooper's empty armor clattered to the ground as the other Imperials stared in disbelief. Eppon took advantage of their shock and attacked another trooper.

"I can't look." Tash shuddered.

"You have to," Zak whispered. "Eppon's growing!"

It was true. Absorbing the troopers made Eppon stronger. Before their eyes, he had another growth spurt, becoming taller and older. But that wasn't all. This final growth must have triggered some other mutation in his body.

As Eppon grew, the purple blotch on his forehead spread

quickly down his face and neck, covering his entire body in thick purplish scales. His head grew huge, his hair fell out, and on his skull, thick veins popped out. His arms, which had seemed human enough before, now grew long and crooked, with thick muscles that tore through the seams in his borrowed jumpsuit. The skin on his fingers cracked and thickened until his hands became claws. His eyes filled with a hungry red fire.

All the stormtroopers had frozen in momentary horror. Only Vader was unafraid. He raised his lightsaber and there was a sharp hum as he activated the blade.

As their leader strode forward, the stormtroopers went into action, too. A dozen blasters fired at once, and all of them struck Eppon.

The energy beams didn't slow him down, though. Eppon picked up another trooper as though he weighed nothing, and hurled the armored soldier at the rest of the troop. The stormtroopers stumbled backward in a clatter of armor, crashing into Vader. The weight of a dozen men was not enough to move the Dark Lord, but the confusion caused by the troopers gave Gog an opening.

"Take me to safety!" he ordered his creation.

Eppon obeyed with blinding speed. He picked Gog up in one arm and raced away, moving so quickly that, by the time Vader had shrugged the troopers off, his two opponents were nowhere in sight.

Vader growled through his breath mask. "You've just signed your death warrant, Gog."

Still hiding just inside the cargo ship, Tash, Zak, and Deevee remained utterly still.

"Maybe," Tash whispered as softly as she could, "he doesn't know we're here. Maybe he'll go after Gog and forget about us."

It seemed as though her wish would be granted. Outside the ship, Vader issued orders to his dazed stormtroopers. "Send a squad to search the surrounding area. If Gog and his creature are nearby, I want them alive. Then bring me a report on the location of those Rebels. I want to make sure they do not escape either."

Yes, Zak and Tash thought at the same time. *We're going to make it!*

"But first," the Dark Lord said, turning and staring directly at the cargo ship, "bring the two children and the droid to me. I plan to question them. Personally."

CHAPTER

Darth Vader ignited his lightsaber and held it close to Zak's throat. The energy sword hummed threateningly. "Do you know what this can do to human flesh?"

Zak nodded.

Vader turned to Tash. "Do you understand that I have another, more terrible weapon at my disposal?"

Tash knew that he meant the dark side of the Force, and she nodded, too.

Tash and Zak were sitting on the floor in the cockpit of the cargo ship.

The stormtroopers had dragged them out, searched them for weapons, then thrown them back into the ship for questioning. They'd been locked into the cockpit, where they had waited for almost half an hour while the troopers plugged into Deevee's computer brain and scanned his memory banks. No one had spoken to them. Finally, the door to the cockpit had opened, and Darth Vader had entered.

"Excellent," Vader said. "Then you will cooperate completely."

Zak and Tash both nodded.

Vader's mere presence was enough to weaken even the bravest heart. He was ruthless, and when he focused his terrible mind on them, Tash felt dark ripples of the Force wash over her, threatening to drown her in pure evil. Beside her, Zak felt Vader's cruel will like a shadow darker than anything the wraiths could create.

They told him everything.

They told him about Hoole and his secret past. Vader seemed to know about this already, and did not care much about the Shi'ido. They told him about the Rebels, Luke Skywalker and Han Solo and Princess Leia. Vader was more interested in them, but he already seemed to know more than they did, and he quickly changed the subject.

They told him everything they knew about Gog, but again, the Dark Lord already seemed far ahead of them, and dismissed their words.

They told him how they had first arrived on the planet D'vouran, and discovered the first part of Gog's experiment. Vader seemed eager to hear this, and ordered them to continue. He listened as their story wound its way through all the planets they had visited, all the discoveries they had made about Gog and Project Starscream. Vader was intrigued by the details of each experiment.

Tash and Zak guessed that Gog had kept the details hidden, hoping to keep the experiments for himself. Vader now absorbed every bit of information they could give him about the various sections of Project Starscream. Fearing for their lives, Zak and Tash cooperated.

Except for one thing. Instinctively, neither Zak nor Tash mentioned Tash's growing sensitivity to the Force. They did not mention her frequent intuitions of approaching danger, and they certainly did not mention what had occurred on the abandoned space station known as Nespis 8, where Tash had finally become fully aware of her ability to use the Force.

Tash didn't know what made her leave out those details. Maybe it was the Force itself. But she knew that Vader, once he suspected her awareness of the Force, would never let her out of his sight.

She was sure that Vader would discover her secret anyway. After all, he had been a Jedi Knight before turning to the dark side of the Force. He could sense other Jedi.

But either Tash's Force-sensitivity was very young and weak, or Vader's mind was distracted by other thoughts. He never guessed at the truth. Having gathered all the information he could, the Dark Lord simply turned and strode from the cockpit, locking the door behind him.

A few minutes later Deevee joined them, stumbling into the room as he dragged one useless leg behind him. He was still active, but his chestplate had been pried open and some of his wiring had been damaged.

"Inhospitable brutes!" the droid moaned. "I tried to help them so that they would do as little damage as possible, but they deactivated me! When I was turned back on, they had done this! My left arm is malfunctioning, and my leg servos barely function."

Zak checked the damage. "These wires are blown." He looked around the cockpit. The stormtroopers had locked them in there because, thanks to Gog's blaster fire, the cockpit was useless. The ship was too damaged to fly. The console had been blasted, and loose wires and melted computer terminals were all that remained of the control panels.

"Maybe I can use some of this scrap to repair you," Zak offered. Using his bare hands, he tore a few lengths of wire from the shredded control consoles and began working on Deevee's circuits.

Meanwhile, Tash sat huddled in a corner, her head in her hands. The other two left her alone for several minutes before Deevee finally asked, "Tash, are you all right? Did those Imperials hurt you in any way?"

Tash looked up. "No, I'm okay, Deevee. To tell you the truth, I was thinking of Uncle Hoole."

"Me too," Zak put in. "I just . . . I'm confused. I don't know how to feel. I mean, we owe him a lot, and I know it was an accident, but I can't stop thinking about the fact that he destroyed this whole planet. Millions of people wiped out, just like that!''

"Just like Alderaan," Tash whispered. "Accident or not, it was a terrible thing to do."

"Well," Deevee said indignantly, "if there's one thing you two should have learned by now, it's that one should never jump to conclusions."

"I don't understand," Tash replied.

The droid gave an electronic version of a sniff. "Of course you don't. That's because you only know half the story. I learned the other half from Artoo-Detoo's files. I tried to tell you earlier, but we were interrupted."

"Tell us now," Zak said.

"Yeah," Tash agreed, looking around the room that had become their prison. "It doesn't look like we're going anywhere soon."

As Zak continued his repairs, Deevee told them what he knew. "It's true that Master Hoole is Mammon. And everyone knows that Mammon is the scientist who did experiments on Kiva. Everyone also knows that those experiments destroyed the entire planet. But what no one knows is that Master Hoole had no idea of the danger. He thought the experiments were totally safe. It was his partner who was in charge of making sure the experiments stayed within safe limits."

"His partner," Tash repeated.

"Gog," Zak said.

"Exactly. When Artoo plugged into the laboratory's computer systems, he discovered more files. He relayed the information to me before we were separated. Apparently, Gog knew that the experiments would destroy the people of Kiva, but he convinced Hoole that they were perfectly safe."

Zak stopped working on Deevee for a moment. "How come no one else knows this? All I've ever heard is that Mammon was in charge of the experiments."

Deevee shrugged. "If I were to venture a guess, I would say that the Empire hid the truth. They needed someone to blame for the disaster, and they placed the blame on Master Hoole. Gog's name was wiped out of all the records except his own personal files. Those are the ones we found in the fortress."

Tash looked suspicious. "But why did they pick on Uncle Hoole? Why didn't they blame both scientists?"

Deevee was eager to explain. "Now we come to the part that will interest you the most. After the disaster at Kiva, Master Hoole became disgusted with himself and with the Empire. He decided to work for them no longer. Gog, apparently, continued to work for the Emperor, so the Imperials protected him, while at the same time purposely destroying Master Hoole's reputation."

Zak started working on Deevee's wires again. "Why didn't Uncle Hoole tell us this?"

Deevee explained. "I suspect that Master Hoole still blames himself for what happened to the Kivans. He is too proud to lay the blame elsewhere. He still accepts responsibility for what happened, even though Gog is really to blame.''

Tash wavered. Long ago she had been suspicious of Hoole. Then she'd become convinced that he was on the side of good. Now, her faith in him had been shattered. She wasn't certain what to believe. "Are you *sure* Hoole quit the Empire? What happened to him after that?''

Deevee didn't know. "There is no record. It seems he simply wandered the galaxy. He dropped his first name, for by that time the Empire had spread the word that a Shi'ido named Mammon had wiped out an entire species.''

''Four years,'' Tash muttered. ''When Zak and I broke into Uncle Hoole's personal records we found a period of four years that were totally blank.''

''Exactly,'' the droid confirmed. ''But I think Master Hoole realized he could not wallow in guilt forever. He decided to put his energies to good use. Knowing he could never change what had happened, he swore that never again would a civilization be lost. He became an anthropologist, traveling from star system to star system, gathering information about hundreds of cultures.''

Zak guessed the rest. ''But he must have learned something about Gog, maybe that Gog was using the same technology they had developed to start new experiments. He tried to put a stop to it.'' He looked at his sister. ''That's how all this got started.''

Tash felt tears well up in her eyes. ''He was trying to

make up for what he had done," she concluded. "He's been trying to make sure that no one ever misuses science again."

Deevee nodded. "I would say that, rather than being a figure of evil, Master Hoole has acted quite bravely these last few months."

"He's been acting like a hero," Zak agreed. "And we treated him like he was a criminal."

"It won't matter," Tash said. "The wraiths are going to execute him. He may be dead already."

Deevee rocked back and forth in frustration. "If only we could get out of here and find him!"

"Would it matter?" Zak wondered. "When we left him, it seemed like he was ready to face whatever punishment the Kivans gave out. Even death."

Deevee shook his head. "I know Master Hoole quite well, Zak. I'm sure that we can convince him his life is worthwhile. All we have to do is show him we believe in him."

"All right, then," Zak decided. "Let's go find him."

"And how exactly should we do that?" Tash scoffed. "Just ask the stormtroopers if we can go out for some fresh air? The door is locked, there are stormtroopers on guard outside, and then, of course, there's the little matter of trying to walk out of an Imperial camp."

Zak grinned at her. "The door is no problem. I can hot-wire it by borrowing a little power from Deevee's internal power source . . . and this!" Zak held up two wires he had been connecting to Deevee's circuits. He touched the wires together, igniting a shower of sparks.

"Oh, goodness!" Deevee said as the electrical feedback gave his systems a jolt.

"As for getting out of camp," Zak continued, "we won't walk. We'll fly the *Millennium Falcon*!"

"Your brain's in hyperspace," Tash retorted.

"You always wanted to be a pilot, didn't you? And I've always wanted to get another look at the *Falcon*'s engines. Together, I'm sure we can figure out how that ship works."

"Okay. That's two out of three," Tash challenged. "But what about the stormtroopers?"

A gleam filled Zak's eye. "That's where you come in."

He explained the rest of his plan.

A few minutes later, Tash stood at a tiny round viewport in the middle of the locked door. Through the transpari-steel, she could just see the two stormtroopers who guarded the cargo ship.

"I don't think I can do this," she whispered.

"Sure you can," her brother encouraged. "Just have a little confidence."

Tash shook her head. She didn't need confidence. She needed an instruction manual.

Zak's plan called for Tash to use the Force to trick the

two stormtroopers. Tash had only recently learned that she *had* Force-powers. She still had no idea *what* those powers were, or *how* to use them.

"Here goes nothing," she muttered.

Tash took a deep breath and tried to relax. She had read a lot about the Jedi, and all the books she'd read had said that the Force flowed around all things. It wasn't a matter of *making* the Force do something. It was a matter of *letting* the Force do something. The Force was everywhere. All she had to do was give it a channel.

Focusing her mind, Tash looked at the two troopers and sent a single thought shooting into their brains.

Nothing happened.

She took another deep breath and kept focusing.

Although no one had spoken, one of the stormtroopers looked at the other. "What did you say?"

The second stormtrooper grunted, "I didn't say anything."

Tash continued to concentrate.

"I thought you said something about me," the first soldier growled.

The second soldier looked at his partner. "Are you calling me a liar?"

"I'm telling you not to talk about me!"

Tash turned away from the viewport. "Now, Zak."

Beside her, Zak held the two wires that were connected to Deevee's chestplate. Touching them together, he jabbed the wires into the small panel that controlled the door.

Sparks flew, electricity crackled, and the panel short-circuited. The door slid open.

Outside, the two stormtroopers were shoving one another. One of them struck the other on the side of the head, sending his partner crashing to the ground.

"Run!" Zak said.

The three prisoners dashed out of the cargo ship, past the fighting stormtroopers, and across the stony ground. By the time any of the other troopers in the Imperial camp saw what was happening, Zak, Tash, and Deevee had reached the ramp leading into the *Millennium Falcon*. As they entered the ship, Zak slapped the control panel, raising the hatch and locking them inside.

"Come on!" Tash yelled. "It's not going to take them long to get in here."

They scrambled into the *Falcon*'s cockpit. The ship's controls were a jumble of old and new equipment welded together. It looked like a disorganized mess, but somehow, they knew, Han Solo had turned that mess into the fastest ship in the galaxy.

"Where are the shields?" Tash demanded.

"Here!" Zak said, throwing a switch.

One of the landing legs retracted. Thrown off balance, the *Falcon* groaned and tilted over to one side.

"Sorry," Zak groaned. "Try this one!"

He threw another switch, and the deflector shield indicators went on to full power, just as the advancing stormtroopers brought their weapons to bear.

Tash ran her hands over the controls. They were like nothing she'd ever seen before. "Where would the repulsor switches be?"

"I recommend that you hurry," Deevee urged. "I believe that dark figure approaching the ship is Darth Vader."

Tash felt herself start to panic. "Think, Tash, think. Han Solo flies this ship. He's kind of arrogant, but he's an expert pilot. Think like him." Tash closed her eyes. She'd already called on the Force once today. She might as well try again. Calming her thoughts, she put herself in Han's place. A daring pilot, probably running from the Empire all the time. He'd keep the engine controls within easy reach.

With her eyes still closed, she reached out with her right hand. Her fingers found one switch among twenty, and she flipped it.

The repulsor engines whined to life, and the *Millennium Falcon* leaped off the ground.

"Excellent work, Tash!" Deevee cheered. "Now if we can only locate the forward thrusters."

"Right here," Zak said. "I watched Han do this the last time we were aboard."

Zak grabbed a control stick and jammed it forward. There was a loud roar and a surge of power, and the *Falcon* rocketed into the sky.

"We did it!" Tash laughed as the ship sped quickly across the surface of the planet. "Now we need to find Uncle Hoole. Does either of you know how to work the scanners?"

"No need," her brother said. He pointed out the viewport. Ahead of them, and below, lay a shallow valley filled with shadows. "That has to be where the wraiths had us."

Zak and Tash worked together to steer the *Falcon* down toward the valley. The ship made a loud thud and bounced twice on its landing legs before coming to a stop.

Even before the *Falcon* had completed its landing, Zak said, "I'll be right back," and ran back toward the ship's engines.

"Not the best landing in the galaxy," Tash grunted, "but it'll do."

Deevee said, "I estimate that it will take the Imperials slightly over ten minutes to get here on foot. We don't have much time."

"Let's just hope Uncle Hoole's still alive," Tash replied.

She and Deevee ran back toward the hatchway. "Come on, Zak!" Tash yelled.

Zak was standing at the ship's engineering station, tinkering with some equipment. "I'm almost finished!" he yelled.

"There's no time for messing around!" she fumed.

"Go ahead. I'll be right behind you!" he called back.

Tash had no time to argue. She and Deevee charged forward and plunged into the shadows.

It was like stepping from day into night. They could barely see, and the farther they walked into the shadowy place, the less light they found to see by.

"I may be able to help," Deevee whispered. Something clicked inside his metallic head, and his photoreceptors lit up, casting a pale light into the darkness. It didn't penetrate very far, but it was better than being totally blind.

Tash could feel the wraiths moving all around her, but none of them attacked. Tash had the impression that their attention was focused elsewhere—toward the center of their dark circle. She and Deevee waded forward, the dim light from Deevee's eyes sweeping back and forth.

"Uncle Hoole!" Tash called out.

"Master Hoole!" Deevee echoed.

There was no answer but the angry whispers of the wraiths.

Tash squinted into the swirling shadows. "I think I see something, Deevee—look over there."

The droid turned his glowing eyes in the direction Tash had pointed. His eyebeams fell on a large flat rock. On the rock, Hoole had been stretched out to his full length. Behind him, one of the wraiths had become solid, and its dark body stood over Hoole.

As Tash and Deevee watched, the wraith lifted a huge rock over its head, and prepared to bring it crashing down on Hoole's skull.

CHAPTER

"Stop!"

The voice came out of Tash, but even Tash didn't recognize it. It was commanding and very forceful.

The wraith hesitated. Whispers whipped around the dark circle.

The child has returned.

Why?

Why interrupt the execution?

The execution!

Kill the murderer!

"No," Tash countered. "You can't kill him!"

To her surprise, Hoole lifted his head from the rock. He said quietly, "Tash, do not interfere. I have lived with this guilt for years."

"But it wasn't your fault, Uncle Hoole!" she argued. "I

know you blame yourself, but it was Gog's fault. Deevee found the records. Gog knew that the experiment would go wrong, but he didn't tell you!''

Hoole sighed heavily. ''I should have known, Tash. I should have realized the experiment was a disaster. I am also to blame.''

''Maybe a little,'' she admitted. ''Maybe it was wrong to experiment with life on someone else's planet. But you didn't know things would go wrong!'' She turned to the wraiths. ''Did you hear me? It wasn't his fault!''

Liarliarliarliarliarliarliarliar.

''We are not lying!'' Deevee replied. ''I can show you all the evidence you need. It's back at the laboratory.''

''Besides,'' Tash continued, ''Uncle Hoole has spent years paying for his mistakes, and he's risked his life to make sure it never happens again.''

But it happened once! It happened here! Because of him. Mammon must die!

''We can show you the real killer!'' Tash pleaded. ''He is still alive. Gog is still alive!''

Nononononono! came the whispers. *Mammon! Mammon must die! We will have our vengeance!*

With a violent hiss, the solid wraith brought the stone crashing down.

But Hoole wasn't there.

The instant before the stone struck, Hoole had shapeshifted into a tiny rock rat and skittered out of the way. He hurried toward Tash, shapeshifting as he ran. By the time he reached her, he was a Shi'ido again, and his stern gray face glowered at Tash.

"Did you say Gog was still alive?" he growled.

"Yes, and he's got Eppon. You were right, Uncle Hoole, Eppon *is* Project Starscream. He's some kind of monster!"

Hoole frowned. "There is little time. We must hurry."

He took Tash by the arm and started forward, but he'd gone only a few steps when something hard and invisible flew out of the darkness, hitting him on the chest. Hoole landed heavily on his back.

Noescapenoescapenoescapenoescape! the voices cried. *You will not escape our vengeance!*

Hoole tried to stand up, but a dark claw slashed out of the shadows, drawing a ribbon of blood along his arm.

Tash could feel the wraith's hatred pulsing around them. She knew that even Hoole could not fight shadows. They were going to die.

The wraiths pressed in for the kill.

In the next moment, they were scattered by a blinding flash of light.

Wraiths screamed and fled among the rocks, letting gray light flood into the valley, as though a great black cloud had moved away from the sun. Except that this sun was Zak, who stood nearby with a grin on his face and a small device in his hand.

He held it up. "One of the Rebels must have left this in

the *Millennium Falcon*. It's a thermal detonator," he explained. "Except that I took out the explosives and replaced them with a small ion charge."

"Excellent," Deevee said admiringly. "That worked just as the ion cannon did earlier."

Tash was surprised. "I knew you were good with gadgets, Zak, but how—"

"Hey," Zak bragged, "you're not the only one who reads books. It's just that I prefer tech manuals."

Hoole got to his feet. "We will discuss your choice of reading material later, Zak. For now, we must leave before the wraiths reassemble. Take me to the laboratory."

They hurried into the *Falcon*. For the first time, Zak and Tash sat at the controls, while Uncle Hoole stood behind them. Zak glanced at his sister, who returned his wry smile. So many times, they had stood behind while Hoole led the way. This time, they were in charge.

Their second landing was only slightly better than the first. Hoole leaped out of the hatchway before it had opened completely, with Tash and Zak close behind him.

"The place still looks deserted," Tash whispered.

"Let's hope so," Hoole replied.

They reached the front door of the fortress. All was dark and silent inside. Creeping as quietly as possible, they made their way down the hallway, until they reached the central chamber.

The room looked undisturbed. The doors to the room stood open, since they had been damaged by the Rebels earlier. The enormous command chair still faced the bank of video monitors, its back toward them. Beyond, the door to the egg chamber was still open.

"Okay, we're here," Zak said softly. "Now what?"

"Now," Hoole replied, "we look for any information that might help us destroy Gog's monster."

"Let me save you some trouble."

The voice was high-pitched and shrill—a weird combination of evil pleasure and utter hatred.

The command chair in the center of the room swiveled around, and they saw Gog grinning at them. He looked confident and secure. Even though his laboratory had been abandoned and damaged by Rebels, it was still the center of his power.

"Let me save you some trouble," Gog repeated. "There is no way to destroy my creature."

Hoole's face was stern and threatening. "Then surrender him to me, Gog. I won't let you use this creation to hurt anyone elsc. Give him to me."

Gog smiled again. "Why, of course, Hoole. He's right behind you."

CHAPTER

They spun around to see Eppon looming over them. Even Hoole let out a cry of alarm.

Eppon no longer looked even vaguely human. He was over two meters tall, and covered in purplish scales. The remnants of the jumpsuit he'd worn hung in tatters around his waist. His thick arms reached almost to the floor. His eyes were blood red, and his mouth had become a slavering, tooth-filled maw.

"Eppon—" Tash started to say.

Eppon roared and lunged forward.

They backed away as Hoole put himself between Eppon and the others.

"Don't let him touch your skin, Uncle Hoole!" Zak warned.

Hoole shimmered for a moment, and suddenly a huge

Wookiee stood in his place. The Wookiee snarled. Eppon roared in reply and lunged forward, and the two huge figures crashed together.

Tash and Zak cringed, waiting for Hoole to turn to jelly . . . but nothing happened. Eppon clung to the Wookiee, trying to touch exposed skin, but he could not dig past the thick layer of fur that covered the Wookiee's body.

"The creature can't absorb him!" Deevee realized.

Eppon was as surprised as Zak and Tash. That gave Hoole the upper hand. Powerful blows from his Wookiee claws rained down on Eppon, beating the monster back. Tash and Zak thought Hoole would actually win, until Eppon changed his tactics. With brute force, he started to trade blows with the Wookiee.

A powerful blow of Eppon's arm crashed down on the Wookiee's head, stunning Hoole. Losing his concentration, Hoole shimmered and shifted back into his own shape. Quickly, Eppon grabbed hold of Hoole's arms. Then Eppon's flesh began to ooze and slither. Strings of slime grew out of his skin and started to crawl up Hoole's arms toward his open mouth and his eyes.

"Ooze," Tash said with a shudder. "Just like the virus creatures we saw on Gobindi."

Struggling to escape, Hoole fell on his back with Eppon crashing down on top. As the strings of slime touched Hoole's bare skin, the Shi'ido cried out in pain and fear.

Just then, a black shadow fell across the two combatants. An incredible force lifted Eppon up and hurled him against a nearby wall. Eppon struck the wall with such force that the entire building shook, and the ceiling above them cracked.

Darth Vader had come.

Vader glanced down at Hoole. "You are fortunate that I have not yet questioned you."

Sitting in his command chair, Gog shrieked like a madman at Eppon. "Kill Vader! Kill Vader!"

Eppon leaped to his feet and threw himself at Vader. He slammed into the Dark Lord with the sound of a mountain falling. Vader took half a step back to keep his balance, then lifted Eppon up over his head. Eppon tried to clasp his opponent, but Vader's armor covered every inch of his skin. With the help of the dark side of the Force, Vader sent Eppon crashing into the egg chamber, ten meters away.

Schrrrummmmm!

Vader ignited his lightsaber.

Zak and Tash stared, entranced by the battle, until Hoole and Deevee touched their shoulders. "Run," Hoole said quietly.

They turned toward the exit, but before they could take even one step, the doors crashed closed.

"What!" Zak cried in surprise, pounding on the heavy metal. "I thought the doors were broken!"

They turned back around to see that Vader had momentarily focused his attention on them. He had used the Force to shut them in. "You will not escape me this time. When I have finished with this creature, I will deal with you."

They watched Vader stride toward Eppon, who was just climbing out of the wreckage of the egg chamber. Eppon tried to grab Vader, but the Dark Lord slashed with his lightsaber, cutting off Eppon's right arm just above the elbow. Eppon howled in pain and backed away a step. Even as he did, his right arm quivered and shifted, and a new arm quickly grew to replace the one he'd lost.

"What shall we do?" Deevee moaned. "Whoever wins this fight will turn on *us* next."

Zak was still pounding on the door in frustration.

To his surprise, someone on the outside pounded back. "Let us in!"

It was Han Solo.

"Vader sealed the door. We can't get out!" Zak called back.

Han's voice leaked through the heavy door. "Get back! We're going to blow it open!"

Zak and the others hurried away from the door and crouched down.

Meanwhile, Eppon had grabbed Vader again. This time the Dark Lord did not hold back. He called on the dark side of the Force and used it to lift Eppon five meters into the air. With a strangled cry, Eppon hurtled like a missile straight at the command chair where Gog sat, knocking him over with a loud crash.

Then, *BOOM!* The door was blown inward and flame and smoke poured into the room as the Rebels set off several explosive devices.

113

The heavy door flew across the room and crashed against the wall near Darth Vader.

The echoes of the explosion died, but a deep rumbling continued. "The walls!" Hoole warned. "Watch out!"

The walls had been weakened by Vader's battle with Eppon. The Rebels' explosion had weakened them further. A large section collapsed inward, and part of the ceiling came crashing down as Zak, Tash, and the others used their arms to protect their heads from the falling debris.

When the dust had settled, Tash realized that they were doubly lucky. Rubble covered the far end of the room, making an impassable barrier between the egg chamber and the laboratory.

"Vader's sealed in there!" she cried. "He's trapped in the egg chamber!"

Nearby, Gog had climbed to his feet. Beside him, Eppon panted and drooled. "It won't help you," the evil Shi'ido said. He motioned Eppon forward. "You are still doomed!"

"Not if we can help it," Leia said.

The Rebels surged into the room. Han, Luke, Leia, Chewbacca, and the remaining Rebel commandos aimed their blasters and fired, pouring energy beams into Eppon's grotesque body. The creature squealed as he was struck again and again. He spun around, and collapsed on the floor.

"Cover him!" Leia ordered, pointing at Gog. "Check the creature."

Most of the commandos kept their blasters trained on

Gog. The evil Shi'ido merely grinned and did not move. He leaned forward, eagerly waiting for what he knew would happen next.

One of the Rebel soldiers crept forward. Eppon's purple body lay unmoving, his lifeless face pointed toward the ceiling and his eyes closed.

The commando jabbed Eppon with the end of his blaster rifle.

No movement.

"All clear," he called out. "The creature is—*uurrk!*"

He could not finish his sentence.

Eppon had reached up and grabbed him by the throat.

CHAPTER

No one could move quickly enough to save the Rebel commando. Eppon grabbed the soldier by his bare hands, and the soldier turned to jelly before their eyes. Seconds later, the commando's body had been sucked into Eppon.

The creature leaped to his feet, looking stronger than ever.

The Rebels fired again. The blaster bolts burned gaping holes in Eppon's body, but hardly made him flinch. They did slow him down, though. Instead of charging, Eppon stalked slowly forward.

"Can't this creature be killed?" Luke wondered.

"No," Tash said as the last pieces of the puzzle suddenly came together for her. Eppon was the end result of Project Starscream. All the terrible experiments they had discovered were elements of the project. Each one reflected some part of Eppon's power.

"Just like the undead on Necropolis, he can't be killed!" Tash explained quickly. "He's like all the creatures we've faced! Like the virus creature on Gobindi, he absorbs his victims. And he grows stronger with every creature he eats, just like D'vouran!"

"Sounds like we're in trouble," Han said, still firing at the approaching creature. "We can't hold him off forever!"

Although the Rebel weapons did not stop Eppon, the blaster shots came so fast and furiously that they prevented the creature from coming too close. Again, Eppon changed his tactics. His red eyes flashed, and one by one he gazed directly into the eyes of the Rebel fighters.

"I don't want to fall, I don't want to fall!" one commando pleaded, as though he were hanging from a steep cliff.

"I don't understand," Deevee said in confusion. "He seems to be afraid."

"That's it, Deevee," Zak guessed. "Eppon has the same powers as the Nightmare Machine. He's gotten inside their minds. He's attacking them with their worst fears."

Han, Leia, and the others were soon in the same state, cringing in fear and crying out at things no one else could see.

Luke Skywalker was on his hands and knees. He seemed

to be fighting hard against something. He whispered over and over again: "Ben! Ben!"

Leia dropped her blaster. "No, the Rebellion can't fail. It can't!"

Han had fallen to his knees. "I'll pay you back, Jabba," he muttered to himself. "I'll pay you back, I swear it!"

Beside him, Chewbacca was growling angrily, trying to fight off some Wookiee fear.

Even Hoole fell under its spell. He rocked back and forth, his arms clutched about his shoulders, whispering apologies for the destruction of Kiva.

Only Deevee, Zak, and Tash were unaffected.

Eppon stalked closer. He would be on them in a few minutes. Zak backed up until he was right next to his sister. "We can't fight what we can't even touch!"

Tash, too, backed away, and bumped into Luke Skywalker. Luke had managed to get to his feet. His eyes were squeezed shut as he tried to fight off the illusion. He muttered to himself, "The Force . . . got to stay . . . with the Force."

"That's it!" she realized. "I can use the Force!"

Zak understood. Through his experiments, Gog had managed to take control of the galaxy's most powerful elements. He had learned to control life and death. But the one thing he had never been able to do was control the Force.

"I just hope you can use the Force as effectively as Vader did," Deevee said frantically.

118

As soon as she heard those words, Tash knew that Deevee was wrong. She did not want to use the Force the way Vader had. That was the dark side.

She recalled Luke's words: *The Force isn't a weapon like a blaster or a lightsaber. It's more like a power that helps you focus yourself and understand everything around you.*

If the Force connected all living things, then maybe it connected her to Eppon, too. Maybe she could use it to reach him.

"Eppon," she said softly. As she spoke, she reached out with her feelings, trying to imagine an energy field that flowed from her to the monster and back again. "Eppon, it's me. Tash. The one who took you from that egg chamber. I carried you on my back. We laughed and played together."

Eppon lunged forward to grab her. Tash didn't move. She ignored her pounding heart. She focused on the Force.

"We don't want to hurt you, Eppon. We're your friends. Remember?"

Eppon's clawed hand hung over Tash, but did not come down. He could have destroyed her in a moment, but instead he only growled at her, gnashing his teeth.

Using the Force, Tash connected herself to Eppon's mind. She felt anger, even rage, but somehow she knew that those emotions didn't belong to Eppon. They belonged to the evil scientist who had created him.

She said softly, "What you're doing is not your fault. You were created by evil. But there is good in you. I can feel it."

Eppon lowered his clawed hand.

A few meters away, Gog howled in frustration. "No, no! Destroy her!"

Eppon responded to Gog's command. His red eyes flashed, and Tash felt a wave of cold fear wash over her. Her concentration started to break. She suddenly began to worry that the others would escape while she was fighting Eppon. They would abandon her, leaving her to die while they escaped to safety. They would betray her.

She started to lose her connection to the Force.

Eppon growled, and raised his claws again to strike her down.

You're not alone, Tash. Tash didn't hear the voice with her ears. She heard it inside her head. *You're never alone.*

The sound of the voice made her feel stronger. She concentrated again, and felt the Force flow through her once more.

There was something more. She felt someone else using the Force, too. Someone had added their strength to hers.

Nearby, Luke had regained control of himself. She could feel him concentrating along with her.

Tash aimed all her thoughts at Eppon. She summoned all the images of the baby boy Eppon into her brain, recalling how she had held him, and played with him, and hugged him when the commandos wanted to desert him.

120

The images penetrated Eppon's angry mind. He lowered his claws again. His flaming eyes studied Tash, then turned to look at Zak. He growled softly.

Gog shrieked, "Kill them now!"

Eppon roared again, but this time he did not attack Zak and Tash. The creature whirled about and started toward Gog, its massive arms reaching out to crush him.

"Get him, Eppon!" Zak cheered.

As Eppon approached, Gog raised a small, flat object and pressed a single button.

Eppon's head exploded.

CHAPTER

The creature's body slumped to the ground. His head had disintegrated in a flash of light.

Gog shook his head. "Did you think I learned nothing from my past failures?"

He stood over Eppon's body and kicked it with his toe.

"Learning from mistakes is the basis of all science," he said. "I knew that once I had created the invincible soldiers for my Army of Terror, I had to be prepared in case I lost control." He patted the small device in his hand. "I planted a tiny explosive device in the creature's brain. It was the only way the creature could be destroyed."

"You killed him!" Tash cried.

"Murderer!" Zak spat.

Gog only shrugged. "I created him. He was mine to destroy."

"But you've still lost, Gog," Hoole said. "You'll never get off this planet."

"Oh? Who will stop me, Hoole?" Gog laughed.

"We will," Han said weakly. Beside him, Chewbacca snarled. The Rebels were recovering from Eppon's fear power.

"You? You have more important things to worry about."

Even as Gog spoke, Hoole and the others felt a shadow fall across them. No, not one shadow—thousands of shadows.

The wraiths were rushing into the laboratory.

They filled the room with swirling darkness, whispering and moaning, *Murder! Death to Mammon! Death!*

Zak and Tash felt the wraiths smother them, holding them down, while more of the shadow creatures pinned Hoole in place. He struggled, but could not move. The wraiths surrounded the Rebels.

It didn't matter, Zak realized. They had no ion weapons. They had nothing with which to fight the wraiths.

They all seemed too exhausted to fight. They waited for the shadow creatures to take their revenge.

Except for Deevee. The droid struggled against the shadows that imprisoned him. Calling on every spark of energy that his mechanical body could muster, he pushed his way toward the center of the room.

"Deevee, what are you doing?" Zak asked.

Deevee couldn't spare the energy to answer.

Mammon must die! Mammon must die! the voices moaned.

A black claw slashed through the darkness, ripping a long red line across Hoole's chest. Gog cackled gleefully.

Deevee reached the control console in the center of the room.

Another black claw cut Hoole, drawing blood on his cheek. Gog cheered.

Tash and Zak watched Deevee punch commands into the computer console. In response to his instructions, the console lit up, sending power to the five video monitors that hung overhead.

Gog's image appeared on all five screens.

It was an old recording, blurred by years of electronic storage. But it clearly showed Gog transmitting a message to the Emperor himself.

"Your Excellency," Gog said in the message. "I have completed the final arrangements for the experiments here on Kiva. As we suspected, our experiment is a failure. It will not create life. It will destroy life. However, I plan to let the test go forward. I suspect that the results should be quite devastating, and may provide you with a useful weapon."

The recording ended.

The room was utterly silent.

Then the whispers started. *Gog.*

Another voice joined the first.

. *Gog.*

More voices joined in. The wraiths seemed to be debating among themselves. For a moment, the voices of the shadow creatures were filled with doubt. They had been cursing the name of one scientist for twenty years. It was almost impossible for them to change course now. But Deevee had set the tape on replay, and Gog's recorded voice echoed throughout the chamber: "I plan to let the test go forward."

Suddenly, a thousand voices accused: *Goggoggoggoggoggoggog!*

Gog backed away, pointing at Hoole. "No, no. *He* is responsible. He did it!"

You are a murderer! You are a killer! Gog, you must die!

The shadows fell away from Zak and Tash. They fell away from Hoole, and the Rebels.

They poured onto Gog.

The wraiths descended on the evil scientist. They smothered him until he could no longer be seen.

Only Gog's voice could be heard, screaming in agony.

The blackness of the shadows seemed to collapse in on itself, growing smaller and smaller, darker and darker, until finally it disappeared into thin air. Then the screaming stopped.

EPILOGUE

Tash and Zak let a moment of silence pass.

Their nightmares were finally at an end. Gog was gone for good. Project Starscream had finally been destroyed.

Zak was the first to speak. "What do you think happened to the wraiths?" he whispered.

Hoole answered. "They were creatures of energy and hatred. Perhaps, in killing Gog, they burned themselves out."

By now, the Rebels had fully recovered from the fear Eppon had planted in them. Han Solo shook his head. "And I thought things were weird enough hanging around Luke!"

"Are you all right?" Leia asked.

"I think so," Tash answered. "Thanks for your help."

Luke put a hand on her shoulder. "I think we owe you *our* thanks. That creature might have destroyed us all if you hadn't beaten it."

Tash smiled weakly. "I couldn't have done it without you, Luke. Thanks for coming to help us."

"You kidding?" Han replied with a laugh. "I had to get my ship back!"

The roar of the *Millennium Falcon*'s engines still filled the air as a lightsaber slashed through the last of the rubble. The powerful sword cut a large hole through the wall of debris, and Darth Vader stepped into the laboratory.

His eyes, hidden by the dark mask, quickly scanned the scene. He saw the empty room. He saw the corpse of the dead creature. He knew that Gog's experiment was over. The Rebels had succeeded in destroying the first soldier in the Emperor's Army of Terror. Without Gog's knowledge, there would be no others.

Vader felt no regret. Even a creature as powerful as Eppon was nothing compared to the power of the Force. Besides, the Army of Terror was supposed to have been unbeatable, and Gog had been able to destroy his own creature. Obviously, the experiment was flawed.

The Dark Lord turned his thoughts to the Rebels. They had escaped him again. He swore by the power of the dark side that he would find them. Dark thoughts filled Vader's mind as he strode away, leaving only the dry, sad wind of Kiva to sweep through the ruined laboratory.

The wind whispered around the room, swirling in the corners, swirling around Eppon's body.

Maybe it was the wind blowing across the dead planet. Maybe not.

But a moment later, one of Eppon's fingers twitched . . .

Hoole, Tash, and Zak continue their journeys to the darkest reaches of the galaxy in *The Brain Spiders*, the next book in the Star Wars: Galaxy of Fear series. *The Brain Spiders* will be available in stores in December 1997. For a sneak preview of this book, turn the page!

AN EXCERPT FROM

BOOK 7

THE BRAIN SPIDERS

"Help!" Zak shouted, leaping backward.

But the spider reversed course on spindly legs that made metallic clicks against the stone floor.

"Relax, Zak," Tash teased. "It's only a spider-shaped droid."

"Yeah," he replied. "But look what it's carrying."

Attached to the spider droid's small body was a glass jar filled with yellow-green liquid. Floating in the liquid was a solid mass of grooved gray matter. A brain.

"It's a brain spider," Tash said. "Remember? We saw one the last time we were here."

"Yeah, but what are they for?" Zak asked Hoole.

"We can discuss them later," Hoole replied. "We are at the throne room."

Their guide, Bib Fortuna, ushered them through the portal and they looked down on a scene of utter chaos.

Jabba's audience chamber was just as Tash remembered it—crowded with aliens from a dozen worlds. There were gangsters, smugglers, thieves, and bounty hunters, all of whom lived in the shadows of the Empire. They hovered around Jabba's throne like dark moons orbiting a massive planet. Whenever anything illegal happened in the galaxy, Jabba the Hutt was sure to be at the center.

Something moved in the shadows nearby, and Zak jumped out of the way, thinking another brain spider had approached. Instead, something far more dangerous stepped into the light.

The bounty hunter Boba Fett.

Zak stared at the killer's helmet, which hid his face. Their paths had crossed once before, on a planet called Necropolis.

"Boba Fett!" Zak gasped. "I—I'm Zak Arranda. Remember me?"

The bounty hunter adjusted the blaster cradled in the crook of his arm.

Zak stammered, "Y-You saved me from being buried alive . . ."

The man behind the mask said nothing. Zak saw his own reflection, twisted and warped, in the face of Boba Fett's helmet.

If Fett remembered him, he gave no sign. Without a word, the killer turned and stalked away.

Zak turned back to the center of the audience chamber.

There, Jabba was talking to the local symbol of Imperial order and authority, Commander Fuzzel.

"He must have left for Jabba's palace right after we did," Tash whispered to Zak.

"Silence," Bib Fortuna warned.

In the audience chamber, Commander Fuzzel stood before Jabba's throne.

"Excellent work, Jabba," Commander Fuzzel was saying. "That's the third criminal you've turned in this month. The Empire thanks you."

From his platform, Jabba the Hutt rumbled a satisfied laugh. Tash noticed that the sluglike gangster looked bigger than the last time she'd seen him. He was growing fat on bowls full of live eels. "I'll take your thanks," the Hutt replied, "but I'd rather have the reward money. That criminal had a huge bounty on his head."

"You'll get the reward," Commander Fuzzel said. "All three criminals were wanted dead or alive, and I notice you turned them all in *dead*."

The Hutt grinned. "They're less trouble that way. I'll expect the money to be in my account by morning. Good-bye, Commander."

Zak turned to Hoole and whispered, "What's a gangster like Jabba doing turning criminals over to the Empire?"

"Quiet," Hoole replied softly. "Listen."

"One more thing," Fuzzel said before leaving the audience chamber. "There's a rumor that the killer Karkas is on Tatooine. I want him. I'll pay double."

"Double?" Jabba mused. His voice sounded like a rumbling stomach. The alien crowd watching the conversation also murmured in surprise. "I will put my best people on it," Jabba replied. "Good day."

This time the Imperial took the hint and turned around, carrying his rolls of fat out of Jabba's audience chamber. As he left, Hoole led Zak and Tash before the throne while Bib Fortuna whispered in the Hutt's ear.

"Well, well," Jabba growled. "What brings you three back to my doorstep?"

"Jabba," Hoole began. Jabba's seedy henchmen leaned forward to listen. So did Zak and Tash. Hoole hadn't told them what he planned to ask. The Shi'ido continued. "Years ago you did me a favor. When I was on the run from the Empire, you managed to erase my name and records from the Imperial networks so that I could continue to move around the galaxy without arousing suspicion." He paused. "I'd like to ask—as a *favor*—if you could do that again."

The crowd rumbled. Hoole had used the word *favor*. It was very dangerous to owe a Hutt a favor, because a Hutt always collected.

Jabba stared at Hoole, and a broad smiled crossed his slimy face. The Hutt's thick pink tongue slithered out and ran along the edge of his lips.

"This can be done," he gurgled, "for a price. I have a job that requires someone with your particular talents."

Tash saw Hoole tense. This was the most dangerous part of the bargain. For years, she knew, Jabba had wanted to get

Hoole on his payroll. The Shi'ido's shapechanging powers would make him an excellent spy, or even an assassin. She shook her head slowly. What if Jabba asked for something Hoole could not—or *would* not—do?

"Relax!" Jabba snorted. "I see the fear even in your stone face, Hoole!"

The crime lord waved toward Boba Fett, who had appeared near the Hutt's platform. "As you can see, I have all the assassins I need at the moment. No, this task is a little more . . . scholarly."

Jabba thumped his thick tail on the stone platform, and Bib Fortuna slithered forward. Carefully, he held up an ancient scroll. Both Tash and Zak gasped. They had grown up on computers, datadisks, and holographic projectors, just like their parents and grandparents before them. Paper books were rare treasures, and something as old as a scroll was almost unheard of.

"That has to be as old as the stars," Tash whispered.

Hoole looked down at the document without touching it. His eyes had barely skimmed the first few lines before they blazed with interest. "Do you know what this is?" he asked Jabba the Hutt.

Jabba shrugged his fat shoulders. "I know it's valuable to the B'omarr monks. I found this scroll—along with a dozen others—in one of their tunnels. They've been begging to get it back ever since."

"*Are* you going to give it back?" the Shi'ido asked.

"Maybe," Jabba gurgled. "But first I want you to translate

it. Translate this document for me, and I'll erase your names from the Empire's computer banks forever.''

Tash had known Hoole long enough to read at least a few of his moods. Although his face was stern and motionless, she could tell by the way he leaned slightly forward, never taking his eyes off the scroll, that he wanted the job.

''Agreed,'' Hoole said after waiting for almost a full minute.

''Excellent!'' Jabba roared. ''It will take a few days to break into the Imperial computer. That should give you time to do your research. Fortuna, show them to their rooms!'' The Hutt thumped his fat tail on the stone platform, dismissing them.

As they left Jabba's throne room, Tash felt dread creep into her stomach, as though they had just made a deal with the dark side.

Fortuna showed them to their quarters. Hoole was given his own room, and Zak and Tash shared a small bedchamber next door. Without wasting a moment, Jabba's servant then escorted them through one of the many dark hallways in the palace. But unlike the others, this one led down, down, down into the cool darkness of Tatooine, far beneath the hot sand on the surface.

''Who are these B'omarr monks anyway?'' Zak whispered in the dark.

Tash clicked her tongue. ''If you read more, you'd know they're the ones who built this place. This was their fortress, before Jabba came and took it away from them. Now Jabba lets them live only in the lowest levels of the palace.''

''I wonder if we'll meet one,'' her brother said.

''Meet now,'' Bib Fortuna said, stopping suddenly. He

seemed eager to get back to the action and intrigue of Jabba's throne room. "I go."

Fortuna vanished into the darkness just as another figure appeared. This one was smaller, and dressed in a brown robe and hood. He was about Zak's height, and when he pulled back his hood, they saw the face of a human boy. He looked about a year older than Tash.

"Greetings," he said in a friendly voice. "Do you wish to visit the B'omarr monks?"

"Yes, we do," Hoole replied.

A grin spread across the boy's face. "Great!" he said in a very unmonklike fashion. Then he said more seriously, "I mean, you are welcome. We don't get many visitors here. My name is Brother Beidlo. But you can call me Beidlo. I will be your guide."

Beidlo led them down a long, curving hallway as he told them a brief history of the B'omarr monks: how they had lived in the palace for years until Jabba arrived. Now the crime lord tolerated them as long as they didn't get in his way. Zak and Tash were fascinated by the things Beidlo said, but Hoole seemed more interested in studying lines of ancient writing that decorated the hallways.

Halfway down the corridor, Hoole stopped.

"These markings are quite similar to the document I'm translating," he mused. "I must look at it again. Zak, Tash, let's go back."

"Oh," Beidlo said, disappointed. "But there's so much more to see."

"I wouldn't mind staying," Tash offered, trying to sound as mature as possible. "I mean, it's not often we get a chance for a guided tour. I'm sure it would be good experience."

Hoole considered. Tash and Zak could almost see his mind calculating how much trouble they might get into on their own. Finally, he agreed. "But keep an eye on a chrono. I want you back in our chambers by suppertime."

With their uncle gone, Zak and Tash picked up the pace of their steps and their questions. Zak couldn't help asking: "Don't the monks want their old homes back?"

Beidlo shrugged. "That's one of the things I don't understand yet. The monks don't seem to care. Every time I ask, they just tell me to push all such thoughts from my mind. I guess I'm just not enlightened enough."

"How long does it take?" Tash asked.

Beidlo shrugged. "It depends on the person. Some monks advance very quickly, but for most of us, it takes years."

"You seem like an awfully young monk," Tash observed.

Beidlo nodded. "I'm the newest member of the order."

"Is that why you get stuck with the job of greeting tourists?" Zak asked.

"That's right. The other monks are too busy with their studies," Beidlo said. "But I don't mind. It's nice to see new faces once in a while. This place gets pretty boring."

"Sounds like Tash's kind of place," Zak grunted. Then he added, "If you don't like it here, why stay?"

Beidlo shrugged. "I don't have anywhere else to go, really. My parents were killed by Sand People, and the B'omarr monks were willing to take me in. Besides, everything's not as dry as the desert around here. Come on, I'll show you."

Beidlo turned down another passageway. "You'll find this interesting. I'm going to show you the Great Room of the Enlightened."

"So, what do you monks do in the Great Room of the Enlightened, anyway?" Zak asked, half-joking. "Dark, mysterious things? Secret rituals?"

Beidlo chuckled. "Hardly. But we manage to keep busy," he said. "We meditate . . . and think . . . and consider . . . and concentrate. It's a full day!"

Zak and Tash followed Beidlo through a wide portal. "Take it from someone who spends every day trying to become one," Beidlo added. "There's absolutely nothing dark, mysterious, or wicked about the B'omarr monks."

As he said this, he led his visitors into an enormous room. Shelves lined the walls, but Zak and Tash's eyes were drawn to a crowd of brown-robed monks standing around a table.

As soon as the newcomers entered, the monks whirled around to face them. Angry eyes glared from beneath their hooded cloaks. One of the monks was holding something close to his body. Seeing what it was, Tash and Zak both gasped.

In his cupped hands, the monk held the squishy gray blob of a human brain.

ABOUT THE AUTHOR

John Whitman has written several interactive adventures for *Where in the World Is Carmen Sandiego?*, as well as many Star Wars stories for audio and print. He is an executive editor for Time Warner AudioBooks and lives in Los Angeles.